THE *Smoke* FREE ZONE

NIGEL GEARING

Mereo Books

1A The Wool Market Dyer Street Cirencester Gloucestershire GL7 2PR
An imprint of Memoirs Publishing www.mereobooks.com

THE SMOKE-FREE ZONE

First published in Great Britain in 2019
by Mereo Books, an imprint of Memoirs Publishing

The address for Memoirs Publishing Group Limited can be
found at www.memoirspublishing.com

The Memoirs Publishing Group Ltd Reg. No. 7834348

Typeset in 9/12pt Bembo
by Wiltshire Associates Publisher Services Ltd.
Printed and bound in Great Britain by Biddles Books

"The imagination is always at the end of an era."

Wallace Stevens

PROLOGUE

Lines and circles, loops and diagonals. The City as circuit-board, the Calendar as helix...

He was looking for a meaning to it all and could find none. How appropriate that they should have called it 'the Noughties'!

Perhaps he would begin not where gridpoints converged or timelines crossed, not where some suffered tragedy and others (himself included) went on with their privileged doggie lives. No – not, then, 9/11. Not even four years later, on 7/7, when, as people lay dead and dying on the buses and tubes of Central London, workers like himself trudged home across the streets and parks, some of them noting how along Westminster Bridge and in front of the Abbey, down Birdcage Walk and beside St James's Park, vintage ambulances were lined up in a sixty-year commemoration of the Second World War. His parents' war. Not his own, thank God.

On this day halfway through that decade, he fancied, a lionised theatre director might have left his wife for another woman...

On this day a 30-something American actress who had herself enjoyed a ringside view of the falling Twin Towers might have decided she would henceforth pursue academic interests in the UK...

From his hill-top eyrie he could hear the taverna on the beach below embarking on its modest evening revels – the slap of backgammon blocks, the occasional peal of laughter.

No. Draw the circle tighter, he thought. Begin it all later, a year or even fifteen months. He had to start somewhere...

1

"Rise, Sir Zachary."

Zac Slocombe broke out in a sweat. This was meant to be the high point of his professional life, yet he could feel only panic and confusion.

"Rise, Sir Zachary!"

The voice betrayed some minimal impatience, but down here on his knees Zac felt paralysed. Was the obstruction he was feeling merely physical – that dodgy cartilage, dammit, in his knee? Long gone were the days when a youthful Zac had incurred the injury as a college scrum-half, but it still gave him gyp every time – usually sexual – he found himself thus positioned.

Or was it some other malaise altogether?

"Would you care to rise, Sir Zachary?"

The tone had become somewhat satirical. From down here he could not see the Queen's face – assuming, that is, it was the Queen, but then it always was, wasn't it? And now to further confuse matters his peripheral vision suggested a shimmer of blonde hair more like that of Princess Diana, dead these ten years but remembered fondly by Zac at a PR bash for his theatre company. He could recall clearly enough – it was all rather charming – the wry nostalgia she'd expressed for a 'leather-boy' pub in Earls Court, familiar to her from her pre-celebrity days. But surely she hadn't spoken with this light New York accent?

"Rise, Sir Zachary, from this semi-recumbent position."

What had he been thinking of? Of course! This was not the voice of Princess Diana nor of some American but of none other than Lady Bracknell.

"I can't, ma'am."

"You can't? Or you won't?"

"I've been taking these pills. I get them online, ma'am. They're rather unpredictable. If you could only wait a few minutes, I'm sure that..."

And yes indeed. Now he realised his embarrassment was primarily genital. Well, if he couldn't make it go away by simple denial, he thought, there'd always been another solution...

"Ma'am. Perhaps if you'd be gracious enough to permit me just a glimpse of the royal ankle?"

"I beg your pardon?" The tone – if not the accent - was still the fashionable side of Belgrave Square.

"Or allow me to raise your hem just a fraction? Feel her Majesty's calves?"

If answer was given Zac did not hear it, for suddenly he felt a quite extraordinary pain between his shoulder blades. He wished to cry out as now the sword – for so it surely was, the very same that had just now brushed him into ennoblement – penetrated again and again. And yet even at the same moment a more curious thing was happening. In the very midst of this agony, he felt, wondrously, a stirring of his cock beyond routine pill-provoked arousal.

Could it be possible? he asked himself. Was this what they called The Secret Rapture?

Zac woke from his dream undecided as to whether his penis was semi-erect or semi-flaccid. Hey – either way, he thought, it was progress of a sort. But it was a twinge of arthritis that had woken him with its three strokes of regal cruelty.

No matter. He'd see his doctor again next week– a personable charlatan who serviced many in the performing arts and was happy to prescribe anything curative short of morphine pills in his impatience to get on and exchange theatre gossip.

"I was wondering if you'd care for a tea? Or do I see you have other things in mind?"

His partner Iris stood beside the bed, mildly amused at what the sweat-stained sheets, thrown back in the night, now revealed of his manhood.

"Mm. Perhaps later."

She put down the tea with a smile and began to unbutton her nightgown.

"The tea, that is? Later? When I've had a shower?"

So saying, Zac slid off the bed, pretending not to see the disappointment on her face. He had decided to forgo his morning jog round the park and head straight for the bathroom. His bum (of which, considering his age, he had cause to be proud) disappeared behind the en suite glass cabinet.

As he sluiced himself down, Zac tried to process his dream. Sure, he had gone to bed the night before seething that his coeval, the playwright Robert Donniger, was up for a knighthood. "Jammy bugger," he had cursed. But now he consoled himself that his own time would surely come. Had he not recently got that theatre award for Lifetime's Achievement? (The panel-chair was a friend, but so what?) Was he not a byword for directorial wizardry? Had he not magnificently succeeded in the pioneering of new work – usually by women – despite cynical warnings that only by turning around classics (Dead White Males) could one get invited up to High Table? No, Zac consoled himself, things might have panned out a lot worse. His doctor would continue to caution him about that irregular heartbeat (but then what could he do about it, opined the accommodating quack, unaware perhaps that his patient was not helping himself by taking Viagra). He and Iris – his 'Irish beauty' – were successful in bed more often than they were not, and, almost as satisfying, he was the envy of his contemporaries for this and other examples of sexual conquest.

"Phone for you!" It was Iris, tapping on the steamed-up glass of the shower cabinet.

"I'll take it later. Is that Sarah?" He had promised his ex-wife that he would 'come to grips' (whatever that meant – he for one could not say) with their wayward teenage daughter.

"No. She sounded American."

"So then the guy's like, hey, you said you was into anal and me, I say, since when? And he says your words, baby, and naturally I say don't call me baby, it's demeaning. Oh I get it, he says, like you're one of these post-feminists, right? And me, I say Just call it feminist, forget the post, you wanna fuck or not?"

Hadley was finding it difficult to keep up with the erotic adventures of her friend Breeze. She was never at her best before late morning and she had been trying to catch at least some of what was being said by the middle-aged Professor at the front of the class.

"Of course, certain commentators would opine," continued this same Professor, raising an eyebrow in the direction of Breeze's murmur as if behind it might lurk just such a commentator, "certain would opine that the play is an exercise in reification. Making the dead girl a commodity, an object, a thing – call it, excuse me" – he giggled slightly – "Call *her* what you will."

Before carrying on, he fingered his beard a moment. Hadley read it as some advertisement of increased sincerity. "Others again see the play as, precisely, a critique of just this reification. Though written by a man, they see it as a feminist attack on just how a patriarchal consumer culture reduces women to the status of objects. I should say right away that I place myself among these staunch feminists, although of course" – again the slight giggle – "a mere male!"

"Like what's with this asshole?" whispered Breeze before resuming her narrative. "Where was I?"

"Anal or otherwise, feminist or post," said Hadley.

"Right! So he's like, sure I wanna fuck, just a matter of where – front or back. And I'm like, hello?

Excuse me? It's my body you're talking about, dude, not the entrance to an all-night diner."

Once again Hadley tried to tune her out.

"Then again there is a third option," resumed the Professor. "To attribute to this declared 'object' the interiority we know from, say, first-person narratives. To try and see it from her point of view. To give her a name and identity like any other dramatis persona. Here, I think" – and once again he stroked his beard – "we commit a grave error. We run the risk of attributing feelings and emotions which are inappropriate."

"Excuse me."

"Yes?"

Hadley had startled both herself and Breeze with her sudden intervention. "Are you saying it's inappropriate to have feelings and emotions? That this somehow diminishes rather than enriches the girl's status?"

"That is not what I'm saying at all, young lady. Er – Hadley, isn't it?"

Hadley nodded. The class was into its fifth week. The Professor might at least have got more accustomed to their names.

"Not at all, Hadley. Rather I would say that nomination itself – at least in a genre such as this..."

"Er, what is that genre exactly?" interrupted Hadley again.

"At least in a genre such as this, which, whatever else it is, is scarcely nineteenth-century bourgeois realism." This time he managed both a stroke of the beard *and* a slight giggle. "Well, in such a context, nomination is, I think, a false lure. I'm reminded here of something once said by Lacan..."

And effortlessly the Professor embarked on a tactical withdrawal which, as Hadley had feared the moment she had opened her mouth, would consume much of the seminar's remaining hour.

The participants were discussing a British play written some eight years earlier which had enjoyed great critical success at home and on the international circuit. Hadley and Breeze – Americans both, and both currently beached on this academic shore of London – had seen it and admired it in their respective towns of New York and LA. The particular module of postgraduate Theatre Studies for which they had enrolled sought in one of its strands to discuss how this and other plays might most profitably be staged. The module was called 'Whither The Text?' Already Breeze, shaping up fast as the class's self-elected Bad Girl, had whispered her personal answer – "Up your ass, maybe?" – and her ability at one and the same time to follow the lectures, comment satirically on the speaker and recount details of her rich sexual life had never failed to impress Hadley.

As if to underline this, Breeze's mobile beeped in her shoulder-bag. The Professor paused in mid-sentence and looked wearily in her direction. Breeze grimaced an apology; the Professor continued.

"Cool," whispered Breeze, surreptitiously reading a text message. "That director I mentioned? Zac Slocombe? He said he'd see me!"

Twenty years, a past made up of similar wan evenings, a lack of friends, also that defiance and weakness which toward the end of their lives isolate women who have loved only one love, settled them face to face for one more night to be endured while waiting for another identical evening – these two women, each suspect in the other's eyes...

Sarah looked up from her reading and caught her reflection in the mirror. For a moment she saw herself as indeed two women, one scrutinising the other.

She had been reading since six in the morning – nowadays she rarely slept longer – and Colette offered the consolations of good literature and the *roman rose* combined. Was it too early to ring Simon? Then again, had she left it too late? Would he be already on his way to work? The longer she delayed, the guiltier she would feel about cancelling their weekly lunch.

If indeed, she did cancel... She would read on, she decided, for another half hour.

It was her third reading of *Chéri* and *The Last of Chéri* , conveniently bound in the same volume. The first had been when she was a sixth-former, already the school beauty in the eyes of her less striking fellow-boarders but forever and perversely hidden from view, eternally hammering away at the more accessible piano scores of Bach and Chopin. The school 'music room' they called it, but in truth it was a glorified broom cupboard in which to store a battered upright – always slightly out of tune – a couple of guitars and an incomplete drum kit, all dutifully remembered and dusted off when it came to end-of-term celebrations and concerts. A sympathetic teacher had even slipped her a key for her private use.

Sarah's enthusiasm for the piano had not survived into her college years and she wondered now if it had all been a convenient alibi for escaping her 'chums' – for the most part gamey, sometimes hilarious, but perpetually and irredeemably silly. It was about this time, now home from the holidays, that she had caught up with one of the St Trinian's movies where the so-called 'swot' was a ravishing beauty, perhaps the younger Diana Dors. If later she could understand that this was a mild sexist joke – how ridiculous to squander one's prettinesss on fusty old books when one could be out flirting with boys! – she would also remember how even at the time she'd thought the 'glamour puss' in question might be on to something. That same year she'd stumbled upon Colette's shorter novels.

How she had worshipped the wondrous Léa, who seemed to live only for love and champagne! Léa, who was so much wiser than her dishy but shallow younger lover! At the age Sarah then was, Léa's eventual transformation into a stocky matron seemed alien and slightly frightening, and it was only at a second reading – Sarah by now in her forties – that she would marvel at the boldness with which Colette took her heroine into this other phase of life.

Now she herself was close to the age of the final Léa. Though she acknowledged a thickening of the waist and the chin, Sarah knew she was not physically, thank God, anywhere close to her sometime idol's ultimate incarnation. Likewise, green eyes and very fair hair had signalled from the first that she would not decline into the full-faced and ruddy stereotype to which other members of her family – possibly through some rogue Irish gene – had so often reverted. As for her figure, well, she just had to be vigilant.

By the time she had left drama school in London she was a full-blown beauty in the eyes of all except herself. 'Grubby with irregular features' would have been her own passport description. But she had not seemed so to Saul Radzinovic, when she had crossed the path of this already legendary producer. Although a gentle lover despite his abrasive reputation, he was many years her senior and the relationship proved to be as tense as it was short-lived. By the time she and Saul had separated she had produced Mark, who would be her only son, but not as it happened her only child.

Well, Saul was long gone now (he had had the good grace before expiring to provide her with a splendid North London house and Mark with a trust fund) and had been replaced these last twenty-odd years by Zac, golden boy of the theatre, with whom she had adopted Sophie, a Rumanian baby girl now herself about to fly the nest for a course in stage management. When Zac, only four months into their marriage, had proved himself an unreconstructed libertine whose sexual incontinence would not be circumscribed, the adoption had seemed a marvellous way of refocusing their partnership as well as of satisfying that long-suppressed wish for a daughter. In the event, Zac had continued his philandering willy-nilly and Sarah, embittered, had sought both revenge and consolation in the arms of others. Simon was just the latest in a sequence of lovers initiated from that time forth.

Ah, Simon! she thought. What the hell... She threw her book to the floor, picked up the phone and dialled his number. Too bad if he was already in class. She fancied lunch – and she fancied a fuck.

On the other side of London, Simon woke later than intended. For the first time in many months he was remembering Julie. Had he been dreaming about her?

Some twenty-five years earlier, Julie had been his best friend and his intermittent lover. When she had thrown herself under a train, it had been from a broken heart caused by a boyfriend Simon had never much cared for and had never seen since. Had Simon felt responsible in some way? Less than he would have guessed. And yet he had been plagued for months after by dreams. Julie, cropped of hair and baggy of trousers, speaking to him from the other side of smeared Perspex in a prison visitors' room... Julie naked, curled up foetally on a bare mattress beneath a sloping attic-roof skylight... Julie finally absolving him, letting him go by declaring he was not to blame. Thereafter, the dreams had diminished, to be replaced by others more benign.

Was it, he asked himself, the time of year that had produced this surprising retrospective? Each November marked the melancholy anniversary of her death. But why today – or this last night? Simon tried to shrug it off and concentrate on the day ahead.

Soon, and a little more hurriedly than usual, he'd be crossing the park on the way to his eleven o'clock seminar. 'Henry James And His International Theme.' Soon he'd be reiterating those neat polarities which tripped off his tongue like a mantra – American and Europe, Innocence and Experience, Vulnerability and Corruption – regardless of his increasing belief that they were irrelevant to twenty-first-century life. (In his experience young American women were infinitely more street-wise and frank, certainly in matters sexual, than their European counterparts. But then again, wondered Simon, perhaps that was James's point – a certain transparency as opposed to Old World deviousness?)

When he had finished his class, he would catch the Tube to Sarah's house and they would go to lunch in a local though expensive brasserie. Here Sarah would give him news of her children, of her plans to produce this show or that, and after paying for the meal with her customary generosity she would allow Simon to take her back to his flat, ply her with coffee, then make long, drowsy love to her till late into the afternoon.

Or so it had been till recently; lately this last and most agreeable part of the ritual had gone missing. After the last few lunches Sarah had cried off, claiming she must get back to deal with the problematic daughter Sophie (now studying – or rather not studying, hence the problem – for GCSEs) or to pay the decorator, or to be there for some household delivery. Was she planning a new affair? Or was it the anti-depressants she'd been taking, with their allegedly infamous impact on the libido? Simon recognised a certain callous laziness in himself when it came to probing the situation. If the worst came to the worst, he thought, he would just let it go. After all, they'd had a 'good innings'.

They had met some five years earlier at a theatre performance, the fag-end of Simon's brief sortie into the world of thespians. By profession and temperament an academic, he had nevertheless amused himself one summer by adapting for the stage a little-known ghost story by Henry James. It had been no more than a whim on his part, but before he knew it a chum in the university's Theatre Studies Department had asked to have a look, it had been passed on to a director and – lo and behold – there it was, a considerable success on the Fringe before becoming only slightly less of a success on its transfer to the National Theatre.

For a few months Simon had found himself thrown into the world of relatively famous actors and actresses who regarded him – irredeemably 'the Professor' – with a certain ironic affection. There was surely a *quid pro quo* here. An actor in the company who'd once had a film on at the Cannes Film Festival amused Simon with tales of how the jury members who were film stars liked to see themselves as intellectuals, while the occasional intellectuals on the jury – writers, critics, pundits – liked to see themselves as film stars. Something of the same exchange went on now. Was it this that attracted Sarah and him to each other?

He knew her to be an actor (he had quickly learned that late twentieth-century political correctness deemed that all in their profession should be called such, regardless of gender) and that she was wife to some sort of theatrical luminary. When, introduced by a member of the cast, she had invited Simon first to a party at her house and then to a dinner *à deux* – the husband conspicuously absent – he had belatedly picked up the ball. One meal had followed another till he had finally asked her to sleep with him. Once. Then twice. On the third occasion, she had accepted and proved herself a sexual partner of incandescent vitality.

What was Sarah's 'game plan'? Simon had asked himself in those early days. Was there such a plan – or indeed anything beyond the joy of sex? He had come to feel that she had chosen him precisely *because* he satisfied some intellectual need not met elsewhere in her life. But here too, and right from the beginning, lay Simon's anxiety. The academic, the intellectual, the youngish Professor might indeed seem an interesting change from previous lovers (Simon soon learned without rancour that there had been many) but how long before the novelty wore off? How long before the already less than thrilling world of academe bored even an outsider? Who was it who'd said that the partner or consort of an academic was necessarily at *two* removes from all that was most interesting in life?

Simon's mobile rang just as he reached the far side of Kensington Palace Gardens. It was Sarah, inviting him both to have lunch with her after his seminar and to accompany her to a 'wrap party' held by the producer-son early in the evening. And between the two? wondered Simon. Between the lunch and the wrap party?

Later that day Hadley and Breeze were sharing a pastrami on rye in what purported to be an all-American diner just off Covent Garden. Both had concluded that the sandwich, like the diner, was a grave disappointment, resembling nothing they knew back home.

"Hey, I rang Zac," said Breeze, prodding at her plate. "Zac Slocombe? The director?"

"Ah. Right."

"He said he was kinda busy – he's rehearsing a new play – but he'd see me anyway."

"Cool." Hadley chewed on for a moment. "Er... why do you want to see him exactly?"

"The list, honey! The list! *Streetwise*, remember? Just after Christmas? I thought, well, since he *was*, like the director..."

"Right."

"Since he did develop it from scratch with... what's her name?" Hadley supplied the name of a prominent female playwright. "Well – hey," continued Breeze, "just watch the face of Teach when he tries to put us down on the whys and wherefores of that particular piece! Watch that self-satisfied smirk of his disappear when I tell him I've met the Man Himself! *Talked* to the Man Himself!"

Hadley nodded. She, like Breeze, was aware of this director's work method. Suggest a theme to a chosen writer, allow the assembled cast to go off and do their own private research into the world of the play, have them come back and present what they'd gleaned – even, perhaps, improvising certain vignettes – and then leave the playwright some six weeks to fashion a drama which fed off, energised and finally consolidated the collective findings. *Streetwise* had been such a venture, perhaps the crowning glory of a whole series of productions Zac Slocombe had masterminded. An interview with him was rather more than interviewing 'just' a director; he was the begetter, the midwife and – with the writer – the eventual proud parent of each piece.

"He suggested this evening," an effusive Breeze continued.

"Wow. Good for you."

"But there's a problem."

"Yeah?"

"He has to go to a party. His stepson, he said. The wrap party for some movie or other? Said if I could make it, just to turn up and present myself. He'd be there."

"So what's the problem? You don't know what he looks like?"

"Sure I know."

"Then..." Not for the first time, Hadley detected in Breeze a bashfulness that seemed to run counter to her bad-ass-fuck-you-all image.

"Listen," Breeze finally conceded, "I'm feeling kinda, well, like, *awkward*? You wanna come too? Give me some moral support?"

Hadley paused, then nodded assent. Why not, after all? The man was clearly interesting, and then she had a semi-academic, semi-theatrical agenda of her own, undisclosed to Breeze. Back in New York as a struggling actress she had followed courses at the Strasberg school and, reading a review of Zac Slocombe's one and only book (a kind of journal kept during rehearsals of *Streetwise*), she had wondered then, as ever since, what was the crossover between Stanislavski, Strasberg and now this fellow Slocombe.

"Okay. You got the where and when?"

Breeze squeezed her hand gently. They could almost have been two thirteen-year-olds setting out on a first date downtown.

This particular afternoon Sarah had proved as forthcoming as in times of old. They had had lunch and returned to his flat. Now Simon turned Sarah over and penetrated her again, this time from behind. It was always vaginal – she had demurred when early on in their relationship he had proposed anal sex and he'd never mentioned it again – but both of them enjoyed varying their positions, Sarah occasionally on top of him (her full, middle-aged breasts cradled by Simon's outstretched hands like two hanging bowls of fruit) or with Sarah pulled upwards from the missionary position and sitting on his cock, sheathing it in her warm expansive belly while she wrapped her arms around him, breathing in his ear, and he supported her upright back with his hands.

All things considered, thought Simon, they were conventional enough as lovers. With one possible exception. Each time Sarah came she would shout her approval and enjoyment so loudly that Simon knew it reached both up and down to other inhabitants of his building. On one occasion the eccentric but friendly Irishman upstairs had seized his elbow in the downstairs hallway where they often met of a morning to sort out their respective post. "You certainly enjoy your girls, Simon!" he had said with a wink. "First I thought it was some kids larking about. Then I realised!" Likewise on another occasion the usually shy Filipinos downstairs – a youngish couple – had looked at him with what he could only describe as a roguish smile.

Sarah enjoyed their sex together – this much was clear – and her apparent inability not to shout out loud ("Yes! Yes! *Please!*") was something Simon considered almost comic, the least of tribulations. Sometimes he simply clamped his mouth on hers; other times and with an affectionate, conspiratorial "Sshh" he would place a gentle hand on her mouth. But for the most part he let her have her way – hey, was anyone really put out by this? – recognising that it was part and parcel of an unconflicted sexuality much like her ability to time an orgasm to coincide with his. Simon was gentleman enough to delay ejaculation as long as he could, his prick slowly and rhythmically generating, he hoped, the same escalation of excitement in Sarah's cunt. But the moment would inevitably come when he could hold off no longer and, sensing this, Sarah would thrust her pelvis up against his, allow her calves to ride up tightly on his buttocks and clinch him to her, always of course with those same shouts and exclamations.

Oral sex was for the most part rare. Sarah alleged she had never been 'good' at it (what's 'good'? wondered Simon) though she seemed to find satisfaction in Simon pleasuring her – licking her clitoris like an ice cream or, he fancied, tracing out letters of the alphabet with his tongue.

Afterwards, he would slip from the bed, make tea and bring it back to her, nestling his prick against her wet backside.

"Quite a cock, my love," she had said the first time they slept together, her face still turned away from him.

"I'm sure you say that to all the boys."

"I think not," she'd whispered, and glided imperceptibly into sleep.

Notwithstanding this afternoon's renewed pleasures, nowadays an exchange even this brief was not to be guaranteed. At best there'd be a simple "Hey, honey" as he lay back down beside her, her tea unnoticed on the bedside table. Already she'd be half-lost to her afternoon dreams and Simon would be left in solitary admiration of the Miles Davis still playing on the tape deck – from the first almost a fixture of their love-making. As Simon himself slipped towards sleep he would speculate on the musician's endless capacity to run fluting, exquisite variations round a central theme. Was this, he wondered, some aural counterpart to fellatio? Where, if at all, did sex cease to hold dominion?

If truth be told, the party was shaping up to be a bit of a drag, thought Hadley, though, God knows, no expense had been spared on booze and canapés. She and Breeze had duly turned up outside the London hotel in question and been shooed through the doors of the grand reception room after the most cursory of name checks. Breeze seemed to have regained her equilibrium. When a sharp-faced woman with a clipboard had said to her "I only have you down for one..." Breeze had ostentatiously reached for Hadley's hand and declared, "Correction. That's one plus my significant other!" The woman had merely smiled and nodded them in, leaving the girls – for girls they seemed to have become again in this escapade – to suppress their giggles till they could be lost in the cacophony of the gathering.

A man in early middle age was just stepping down from a podium. "So thank you one and all," he was saying, "for your contributions to this lovely movie. In due course you'll be getting invites to the formal preview. And woe betide any who choose not to come!"

There was a smatter of polite laughter and applause, followed by a calculated cannonade of popping champagne corks. Animated conversation resumed as people turned back towards partners and friends. Hadley reckoned she could differentiate at a glance technicians from film editors, editors from actors and actors from producers: the sparks dressed down, the higher echelons of the production team dressed up and the actors, according to taste and age, dressed somewhere in between.

But now Breeze was leading Hadley over to a couple standing near the podium.

"Mr Slocombe? I'm Breeze. I spoke to you on the phone today?"

"Of course. Breeze. You made it then?"

Standing to one side of Breeze, Hadley had time to scrutinise Zac Slocombe and the black-haired, blue-eyed woman next to him – presumably his partner – who was even now squeezing his elbow and indicating that she was off to say hello to someone else. Yes,

Hadley would have placed him in his early sixties, but in good shape.

He turned towards her. "And you are?"

"Hadley. Good to meet you."

"You too, Hadley," he smiled. "You certainly know how to wear a nice pair of trousers."

While Breeze squeaked slightly – a great director and a charmer too! – Hadley did her best to suppress a grimace. As it happened she knew her pants were 'nice' (black leather, bought just off Christopher Street) just as she knew she wore them well. She didn't need reminding by this chancer in crumpled cargoes.

"So, Breeze," said Zac, refocussing his attention. "Tell me what you want exactly." Did Hadley detect the slightest suggestion of a lisp?

"I – we – are going to be studying *Streetwise* in a month or two," said Breeze. "I wondered if I could interview you some time about the play's genesis?"

"I'm in rehearsals right now. The end of an afternoon perhaps. You've got my office number?"

Breeze nodded. "It's in Contacts, right?"

"Then call me any time and leave a message. And, er, this studying, it's where exactly?"

Breeze named the college of London University where they were enrolled.

"You too?" he asked of Hadley.

"Afraid so."

"Why afraid? Don't let's knock academia. Perhaps I could do a workshop for you some time. What do you think?"

"I'm sure we'd be thrilled," gushed Breeze. But already she and Hadley could see the black-haired partner weaving her way back through the crowd. Zac seemed aware of this.

"Okay then. Give me a call whenever." To Hadley's slight embarrassment it was her he was addressing, not Breeze. Only as an afterthought did he seem to include them both. "Er – either of you, that is."

Zac's partner had rejoined them. Rather territorially, thought Hadley, the woman now linked her arm in his, whispered something in his ear and, with a pleasant if slightly unseeing nod, whisked him off.

"She his wife?" asked Hadley when the couple were out of earshot.

"Er... I think she's pretty new. Second? Third? Hey, what do I know?"

"Helluva lot, seems to me."

"Oh, I do my homework," smirked Breeze, and it was her turn to link arms and lead them through to another part of the room.

Zac realised that against all expectation he was rather

enjoying himself. He'd never got on with Mark, whose bash this was, but despite the break-up with Sarah he seemed to be on some kind of eternal guest list from which he would only be eliminated, he hypothesised, when he was dead. This evening's invitation he could have happily ignored like many another, but Iris had been up for it: she at least would meet 'interesting people', as she put it. Well, interesting or not, everyone seemed most agreeable. Mark's mother, his ex-wife Sarah, had granted him a smile from the other side of the room as she stood next to that rather over-obliging academic (Stephen, was it? Simon?) who sometimes accompanied her. Meanwhile, in the gang of actors noisily drinking in the middle of the room were a couple of younger actresses he'd slept with in his time (they seemed now to have left the theatre to take up permanent residence in TV soaps and independent movies like this one) and even they had flashed him friendly greetings. On top of all this was the average-to-good-looking American he'd recently been chatting to – clearly thrilled just to be in his presence – and her even better-looking chum (Hadley, was it?), either or both of whom promised well for the future.

Yes indeed. The world – or *faute de mieux* this room – was peopled by women Zac had fucked, was fucking or would like to fuck. Then again, he wondered, seeing the American girls arm in arm in the near distance, were they a couple of dykes? Curiosity led him to make an excuse to Iris – "Another white wine?" – and move closer.

Now, pulling the scattered circles of bibulous jollity into one more coherent audience, some special event was taking place in front of the long bar. To general applause, a couple of the catering staff had whisked a linen cloth from a kind of font or basin on which was propped upright an ice-sculpture of a man's torso. Cut off at the thighs, the arms and the neck, it flaunted exaggerated pecs and a generous, though frozenly flaccid, penis.

With a flourish, one of the staff now set about pouring a couple of bottles of vodka down the torso's neck while the other member of staff, napkin over arm, gestured theatrically for the ring of onlookers to step forward and partake. For indeed the vodka now began to leak from the chiselled penis and into the basin...

"The iceman cometh" murmured someone behind Zac, but the remark was buried by a whoop as a youngish couple – he in dark suit, black T-shirt and black suedes, she in a strapless cocktail dress – were pushed forward by their friends. Making the necessary sacrifice in dignity – to imbibe you were obliged to crouch slightly and then scuttle forward in a kind of duck-walk to be on a level with the font, not to mention enduring the odd ribald comment on your proficiency or otherwise – the man went first, applying his mouth clumsily to the cock. He sucked an instant, to a yelp of approval from the onlookers, then stepped back with a rueful look of "Well, I did my best", while to general applause he wiped his chin clean with a handkerchief and his partner stepped forward. Again the slight crouch, again the scuttle. This time, however, there was an exaggerated sigh of disappointment from all round: the woman had burst into giggles, covered her face and backed off, shaking her head.

Now the waiters made a more vigorous appeal to those who, by good or bad fortune, were standing closest. By a process of elimination this happened to be Breeze and Hadley. Invited to partake, Breeze merely blushed and turning to Hadley said: "I don't think I can." More groans of mock-disappointment, more exhortation. "Sorry!" said Breeze to everyone and backed into the crowd, leaving Hadley exposed to everyone's gaze and expectation.

She paused for only a moment. "Oh for Christ's sake," she said under her breath, and stepped forward. Clasping her hair behind her with one hand – was this little game so very different after all from drinking at a public faucet? – she leaned down, tilted her head and sucked long and hard on the vodka-cock, aware as she did so that she was giving Breeze and others not so much a lesson in oral sex as in style. Behind her the audience whooped its approval. She swallowed and now tilting her head in the other direction – another, louder whoop was followed by more applause – reapplied herself till finally, adroitly, she flicked her head to one side to prevent the vodka dribbling down her chin. She stepped back. The applause and laughter were now coming from the entire room. Making way for another supplicant, Hadley merely smiled and shrugged as if to say, "Dude, what's the big deal?"

But thereafter it was not the warm applause she would remember – the commendation, so to speak, of the community. It was, between her first and second gulp from the iced penis, the glistening eyes of a man who had positioned himself to take it all in, view unobstructed. The eyes of 'Zac'.

Sarah and Simon had left the party early, Sarah confessing that she felt slightly uncomfortable in such close proximity to Zac's new partner, even though she'd met Iris before and was there with an escort of her own. On the way back in the car she had seemed to Simon withdrawn and irritable, and she had dropped him off outside his flat with only the driest of goodbye kisses.

As he stood at his desk unbuttoning his shirt and kicking off his shoes, Simon wearily surveyed his notes – some years old now – for the rest of the semester and the semester to follow. The Turn Of The Screw. The Unreliable Narrator. The Advance Into Modernism...

He sighed. How he longed for that far-distant sabbatical! But the problem was that one day the joyous sabbatical would be over, work would resume and – how many times had he seen this among his colleagues? – far from being refreshed, the returning academic would find his spirit broken, would now be able to think only of early retirement and some way, any way of quitting the entire game. Pity the man who has had just one glimpse of Paradise!

He turned, and walking back into his living room, he slotted a videotape into his recorder. Made in the early '60s, it was a distinguished black-and-white film version of that same James novella he'd be discussing next week. Rather this, he thought, than read the bloody book again. Was there something about this author, he wondered, that turned one off in middle age? Why should this be when once he would have relished the re-reading? But then again, he sighed, much more recently he would have watched the movie with Sarah, after which they'd have gone to bed and made strenuous love, notwithstanding their earlier afternoon tryst. What was going on there?

Zac and Iris returned from the party in high good humour, each in different ways satisfied at having initiated what they considered 'promising' contacts.

Iris was keen to make love and Zac obliged wholeheartedly until he eventually judged her asleep. Slipping from between the sheets, he put on a dressing-gown and padded noiselessly down the hallway. Not that Iris would have begrudged him this private pleasure any more than her predecessors had...

For Zac, this man of many secrets, nursed one secret he could scarcely conceal from his most intimate women-friends. It lived beyond an innocent-looking door in his flat to which he alone had the key. When on occasion he had been obliged to move house the secret had always moved with him, Zac nervously telling removal men to keep their distance, saying he personally would supervise this most delicate and precious part of the operations. It was to this hallowed chamber that, exhausted from rehearsals or from love-making, he would retire. And indeed tonight was just such a night.

Stealthily he unlocked the door, took a deep breath and entered, careful to trip the lock behind him as he now turned to confront his pride, his joy, his clandestine vice. Was it not at moments such as these that he felt most alive? This, the object of his affections, asked for nothing, could be manhandled, brutalised and abused and yet would still be there next night and the night after, soliciting his attention and, yes, that love he had so rarely received or given elsewhere in his life.

Zac sighed with a deeper inner contentment, and reaching for a remote he pressed a red button. With a readiness to please which he found almost sensual, his huge electric train set sprang into action.

2

"And *voilà*! Chaos reigns. The prison is convulsed by riot, a riot even embracing us, the supposedly safe spectators. We are left asking who cut the cake most trenchantly, Marat or the Marquis de Sade? Marx or Freud?"

This week's seminar was just coming to an end. They had jumped back in time to discuss *Marat/Sade* by Peter Weiss, much aided by a film-version on DVD apparently obtained with some difficulty.

"Thanks be to 'Amazon Dot Com'!" declared the Professor. Withdrawing the film from the machine, he brandished it a moment before turning again to the papers on his desk. Why was it, wondered Hadley, that academics felt the need to put ironic

34

quotation marks around any and all manifestations of consumer culture?

"Bet your ass he's thankful," muttered Breeze to Hadley. "Teach gets to run a movie show for two hours and gets paid for it!"

If the Professor heard he gave no indication, but then he had long since had his fill of Breeze, her just inaudible commentaries in the back row and her mobile. Now he was beginning to allocate presentations for the next term and – aha! – Teacher's Revenge swung sweetly into view.

"Looking at our schedule, I see that *Streetwise* comes first. That is to say after Christmas – if indeed there is such a thing as after-Christmas?"

A couple of students laughed sycophantically. To Hadley's surprise Breeze was one of them, even sitting upright to do so and moving slightly in her chair so she would be in the Professor's eye-line.

"This I thought I'd allocate to... Hadley, if that's okay?"

Hadley had scarcely time to shrug – she was about to add a "fine by me" – when Breeze, much agitated, shifted yet more noisily in her seat, even raising a hand to catch the Professor's eye.

"Er, excuse me," she began.

"Ah, Breeze," said the Professor quickly and with the most charming of ready-prepared smiles.

"Never fear. You are not forgotten!" His smile became positively radiant. "I thought for the session *after* that you might like to take on the challenging case of..."

He named a play of the early 1990s written by a rather dour lesbian whose work, this play included, had come and gone largely unremembered except in university theatre studies. He briefly distributed the other plays on the list like so many Liquorice Allsorts.

"If that's all right then" – already the Professor had turned away, wilfully oblivious to a red-faced Breeze, palpitating with outrage, for whom it was clearly *not* all right – "let's return to our earlier discussion and that stimulating essay by Jan Kott on Beckett. Was it not Antonin Artaud who once wrote..."

As the Professor continued, Hadley, not for the first time, tried to filter out the comments of her neighbour.

"Pig! He knew I wanted to do that play!" snorted Breeze. "Fucking asshole cocksucking pig!"

Simon stashed both lecture-notes and texts back in his case. So far so good. He'd 'done' Henry James for another year – though whether he'd done him justice was another matter. The International Theme, the Unreliable Narrator, yes, but there was so much else left unexplored – for example, James's late-in-life decision to dictate his novels, thereby (and against all expectation) encouraging himself to *elaborate*, not curtail, his sentences, indeed spinning them out to almost Proustian lengths, with the hapless reader left hungry for the dropped second shoe, for the deferred Sense Of It All to finally come home.

Outside the college entrance some of the students were still lingering in twos or threes, usually to light up cigarettes, but for the most part they seemed to Simon remarkably purposeful in their swift disappearance to... what, exactly? Lunch? Another lecture? Some romantic encounter?

Simon, picturing alas only the first of these and then in a reduced form (a solitary sandwich), felt strangely envious. He had seen Sarah the evening before. They had gone to see a film and she had made much of the fact that today she would be doing him a favour by not taking him to some boring fund-raiser she was attending. So be it, shrugged Simon – no doubt there would be other evenings. But then, with James still in mind, he wondered if he had not always been saying just that, always deferring things not merely until the next evening but until the next lover too became some kind of staging-post in a mythical journey towards the Big One, the Perfect Union, the Impeccable Partner. How else could he explain that although he was now in middle age he had never lived with anyone except Julie, and even that in circumstances scarcely orthodox?

One of his more attractive students, name of Annette, waved briefly to him as she disappeared round the corner into Kensington High Street, narrowly avoiding collision with a cyclist. On other occasions Simon had paused to speculate on the almost tribal consensus whereby, here in the early twenty-first century, London cyclists ignored all traffic lights regardless of their display. But on this particular day he was lost to his memories. This had been Emma's favourite turf, largely for its shopping...

Ah! Emma! In some respects she had represented the best of times – all the sweeter perhaps for being times which had not outstayed their welcome. After the self-imposed isolation which had followed Julie's death, Simon had resumed a series of pleasant if scarcely absorbing affairs. At a University reception for increased government and corporate spending (yes, by then even the spurned business community – or at least its cheque book – was deemed worthy of approach!) he had been introduced to a Tory Minister and his frisky, resourceful wife. At least so Simon found her when she subsequently rang his department on a pretext and asked for his number. As one they would relish those evenings when her husband was off awaiting the 'yea' or 'nay' of parliamentary divisions. They would slip away from (say) a dinner party or the second half of *Don Giovanni*, taking to his bed and pleasuring each other in a sweaty, frivolous abandon – the more so, perhaps, for the knowledge that at midnight would come if not the Prince's glass carriage then at least her car back to Pimlico.

It could not last. A General Election returned the same government but forced a Cabinet reshuffle. Emma's husband was promoted (or was that sidelined?) to an EU appointment of 'career significance' and, in a wink of the eye, she was out of his life. Between the lines of her increasingly infrequent letters he conjured the presence of some svelte eurocrat who had replaced him in her affections and her bed. A regular, wry Christmas card became the only reminder of their tender liaison, marking off – each year a milestone – how long ago it had been, how far apart they now had travelled.

One year in early summer she rang him unexpectedly. She was in London 'on a shopping spree' and to see her frail mother, now in a home. She seemed of course a little older, but somehow more compact, her contours firmer. They had a deliciously nostalgic lunch at Wheeler's, apparently accepting on either side that it would have no aftermath, and kissed each other on both cheeks (how European!) as she flagged down a cab back to her undisclosed hotel in Belgravia. Thereafter even the Christmas cards stopped. She was all but forgotten now, lost to him except when – very rarely – his eye was snagged by some passing reference to her husband in newspaper reports of Brussels diktats (fishing rights? trade embargos?) and he hurried on to the arts reviews, the TV listings, those obituaries for which she too, or at least her husband, had become a conceptual candidate. *'But that was in another country. And besides the wench is dead.'*

There had been other affairs, perhaps not so dissimilar, seldom going beyond some two-year boundary-post.

Unique among these had been his one venture into same-sex hedonism. Isabelle was a visiting professor from Toulouse who had come on a semester's exchange to his department. She was a redhead and, true to stereotype, something of a wild card. (Simon tried to remember. What was her specialism? Something about Swinburne and flagellation?) They had quickly become friends, then lovers. One night she had taken him to a party held by one of her London-based compatriots where they had drunk too much and smoked some weed. At the evening's end they gratefully accepted the host's invitation to 'crash' there for the night. There was only one bed. Isabelle and Simon had retired to it even while the host – Jean-Marc – was tidying up after the departure of the other party-goers. They lay naked beside each other until they were aware of Jean-Marc, also naked, now standing at the bed's end with an ironic expression and a hard-on. Isabelle peeled to one side as Jean-Marc joined them. Simon was not altogether surprised to find that his host's attentions were for him rather than for Isabelle, who duly disappeared – as it turned out, lying still naked on a sofa in the next room from which, however, she was able to watch all that ensued...

Simon had lain on his back and soon Jean-Marc had straddled his penis. Simon would remember clutching the man's chest-hair and then his vein-knotted erection; he would remember the shock of stroking a chin which had bristles and the smell of men's aftershave. Jean-Marc and he had ejaculated at more or less the same time, Simon registering the warmth of the other man's fluid as it spurted across his own wrist and torso.

Isabelle eventually rejoined them. "Et alors?" she asked Jean-Marc with a smile.

"C'était bien. Il est pas mal, ton copain."

The next morning Simon and Isabelle had let themselves out, their host no longer in evidence and only a pleasant, slightly jokey note on the kitchen table (addressed to Simon or Isabelle or perhaps both of them) saying they must 'come again'. Hung over in their shared taxi back to separate addresses, Isabelle had squeezed Simon's hand and told him she had never felt such *tendresse* for him as when she had watched him and Jean-Marc *en train de baiser*.

What had Simon concluded from this foray into bisexual troilism? That although he would not wish to deny a strange excitement born of, for him, such unfamiliar coupling, gay sex was not 'his thing'. And, yes, perhaps something more important than this. Isabelle's declaration in the taxi had only confirmed for him a suspicion that, despite appearances and despite who might happen to be fucking whom, three-way sex was always an intimate negotiation between two persons only (in this case himself and Isabelle) and that the third party was a sex-toy who might share their bodies but not their minds.

Isabelle had eventually left for France. Like Emma, she had continued for a while to send affectionate, uninformative Christmas cards. And Simon had begun to wonder if he would ever, could ever fall in love.

Some of these memories preoccupied Simon as, homeward bound, he was crossing the park – only to stop with an audible groan, which brought sniggers from a couple of skateboarders on the adjacent parkway. He had suddenly realised that his teaching duties were not over for the day. Fuck it! He had another class to give. And then there was that bloody student he had to meet!

Hadley sat at a table turned towards the entrance of the Saloon Bar. Native Londoners had once known this grandiose pub opposite Baker Street tube as the Falkland but now – wisely or otherwise in the light of still-recent history – it had been re-christened the Globe; Hadley knew only that it had yet to suffer its evening commuter crush. Maybe this meeting was all a waste of time. Seeking out some theatrical venture which might satisfy her intellectual appetite *and* give herself a meaty part, she had tentatively approached the Professor who led her morning seminars to ask if anyone had pre-empted her when it came to dramatising a particular text of James's involving a secluded house, predatory adults and a child-heiress likely to be killed off for her money. Pleasantly enough (after all, she wasn't Breeze!) the Professor had confessed ignorance but suggested she speak to a former colleague who might know more. He was 'into' James and – hey – had some vague relations with the theatre world. Any good? As Hadley looked at her watch, she was beginning to doubt it.

Hadley recognised him the moment he walked in. At least fifteen years older than herself, wearing a slightly worn, slightly baggy Italian suit, an open-necked Oxford shirt and holding in one hand the sort of scuffed misshapen briefcase which had borne witness to too many books too often, he looked to Hadley a little distracted.

He had good reason. Simon had spent most of the afternoon riffing pleasantly to a class not his own (this was a favour for a fellow-academic) on the detective novel, after putting in some half-hearted research at the nearby British Library for an article he might or might not write on film adaptations of Dickens. In the Judd Street lecture hall he had argued to the assembled – largely foreign academics there on some international year-round programme – that the genre was an inevitable brainchild of the increasingly unknowable, overpopulated metropolis. The fog of *Bleak House* spawned the first professional detective, Inspector Bucket, for only such as he could fill up the gaps in this atomised, anonymous new world, could plot and plod backwards and forwards between lost souls groping in a pea-souper for where they'd come from and where they might be going. In the words of a twentieth-century song, *Oh look at all the lonely people*. It was only too appropriate, Simon was thinking, that en route to this Mysterious Stranger – after the detective novel class, meeting up with her was his second 'good deed' of the day – he should pass that rather naff newish statue of Sherlock Holmes, and that, seen from the other side of the street, the smoke-curled interior of this pub was suggestive of some *fin-de-siècle* opium den.

"Hadley?"

"Dr Heycock?"

"Please, 'Simon'. What are you drinking?"

She gestured to her glass of red wine. "I'm cool, thanks."

"Oh in that case I'll just..."

He leaned on the bar trying to catch a server's attention. Well well, he thought, not your average postgraduate depressive.

Simon sat opposite her. They ran through what Hadley knew these days to be the preface to any such conversation. Why she, an American, was studying over here in the UK. For how long. To what end. Summarily, guardedly, they dispatched the subject of Geoffrey, her Professor, and moved on.

"So – Hadley – this, er, Henry James project," Simon asked. "What did you have in mind?"

Hadley gave chapter and verse.

"You know there was a French film which used this idea?"

Hadley did not, and felt suddenly deflated.

"Don't worry," smiled Simon. "It was a fine film, but – well – kind of free with the material. Director name of Rivette. Some saw it as a lesbian fantasy."

"And you?"

He smiled a little ruefully. "I sometimes think I'm a bit naive. The two girls, I just thought they were good mates."

Hadley had to smile. This guy was really kinda cute.

"Actually," Simon continued, "I reckoned it was more about dreams and reality. Narrative codes and that. But then again" – he smiled – "perhaps I *would* think that. How far have you got?"

They talked on a while, Hadley arguing that with a little bit of tweaking she could maybe salvage this story from its long exile in dusty archives, Simon adding, somewhat wryly, that James's dialogue maybe needed a little 'tweaking'.

"Didn't Geoffrey say you had had some involvement with the theatre?" she asked.

"Long ago. And fairly marginal."

"Then could you recommend somewhere I might send it? *If* I finish, that is."

Again a little digression. This time Simon tentatively offered a check-list of what he called the Usual Suspects – theatres or companies fielding new work.

Another half-hour passed on the state of British theatre, Simon claiming no superior knowledge and

Hadley thinking, Hey, I'm enjoying this, till finally she reached for a cigarette.

"Mind if I smoke?"

"No. Please. Go ahead."

"You won't?"

Simon seemed to hesitate, then declined. He was not about to tell her, this stranger, that he'd once had a friend called Julie who had smoked and that Simon had often chosen to smoke alongside her.

Fifteen more minutes passed before it seemed they'd come to the end of their immediate reason for being there.

"And where are you living, Hadley?"

"Down South. Brixton way. Yourself?"

"Bayswater. Place of seedy assignations. Politicians compromised by, er, 'unsavoury' liaisons."

Hadley laughed. "Are you making this up?"

"To a certain extent." Simon smiled. "I'm thinking more of the late nineteenth century."

"Ah. But then in your own words you *would* think that, wouldn't you?"

Simon laughed, warming to her irony. Why did Brits continue, he wondered, to claim Americans had none? Didn't the likes of Woody Allen build a career on it? Had these same Brits never watched *Frasier*?

"I ought to go," he said. But suddenly a mobile rang in his pocket. Apologetically he turned away.

Hadley surprised herself by wondering, and more importantly caring, who this might be from. A lover? And if so, male or female? Was the guy straight?

Simon shut the phone down. She'd caught only some murmurs. "Last night"... "a nice time"... "you too."

"As I say, I ought to go. But listen. If there's anything else you need, do give me a call."

"I don't have your number."

"Ah." He found a felt-tip and a beer-mat. "And here's my email too."

And with some routine compliments on how nice it had been, he was gone, swallowed up outside by a night which seemed to have descended unknown to either of them.

Why did Hadley feel both warmed and depressed by this meeting? Walking out of the now crowded and smoke-filled pub and back to the Tube – she had allowed Simon a couple of minutes to avoid, embarrassingly, bumping into him again – she realised why. It was a combination of his apparent openness and, well – how should she put it? – something closed-in, something slightly ungiving when it came to the shape and texture of his own private life, maybe no more than his assumption that this pleasant chat would know no sequel. Not once had he referred to anything the least personal (unless you counted his enthusiasm for that

French movie). Even his sign-off compliments gave the impression of someone moving on, maybe killing time before resuming an interrupted itinerary.

And yet there had been one odd, interesting moment. In the last few minutes she'd lit up another cigarette and to her surprise – wasn't the world after all divided into smokers and non-smokers? – after commenting that not many Americans seemed to smoke nowadays, he had asked her for one of her Marlboros. Why should she find this significant? With no immediate answer, Hadley dived into the passageway beneath the Marylebone Road.

As for Simon, he could still taste the tobacco on his tongue. Coming up fast behind it was a certain dryness of the mouth he hadn't known for a long time. Ah well, he thought. An agreeable one-off probably not to be repeated.

He could not have said whether he was thinking of the cigarette or of his encounter with Hadley.

But they did meet again. Unexpectedly, considering what she took to be a certain polite indifference on his part towards Geoffrey, Simon was there at a wine-and-nibbles party laid on by her department. Breeze had cried off ("Excuse me? Crap wine, peanuts and small talk with asshole prof?") and Hadley was left to trade discontents with fellow students, polite platitudes with those of the academic staff who'd bothered to show. She spotted Simon standing by a wall, wine glass in hand. Had he seen her? She threaded through the assembled.

"Simon?"

"Hadley. Hi."

"This your 'hood?"

"Excuse me?"

"This your regular neck of the woods?"

He laughed slightly. "No. I got a surprise invite from Geoffrey." He nodded to where, on the other side of the room, the 'asshole prof' was in animated conversation with a colleague. "He seemed to think he owed me."

"For meeting up with me?" Hadley smiled. "Hey – big reward!"

"You could say that."

"What are you doing afterwards?"

Simon was privately impressed. My, these American girls were so direct! "Nothing much. Why?"

"My turn to buy you a drink?"

"Then let me buy you dinner after."

"No need. I..."

"Really. It'll be my pleasure."

Some time in the course of their supper in a local Italian, Hadley established that Simon was not married, not gay, and if he had 'attachments', well, he was either not letting on or not encumbered by them. A girl can only ask, she thought.

"Simon. Did you come to this party knowing I'd be there?"

He looked her straight in the eyes and sighed a little comically. "The truth is out."

"Then what if I told you I... rather fancy you?" She held her breath as he raised his eyebrows.

"Thank you. Really. I don't know what to say."

"Are you going on anywhere now?"

"You mean – after this?" He gestured to the restaurant, its small number of clients. "No. Nowhere."

"Then can I come nowhere with you?"

They went back to Simon's flat. There was some business about further drinks, Hadley accepting a white wine without enthusiasm, then conversation ground to a halt. Was the guy merely shy? A moment passed. The moment, Hadley surmised, where you can throw it all away by referring to tomorrow's 'pressing commitments'. The moment where something lovely can die...

She put her glass on the coffee table and stood up, looking towards the hallway and the bathroom off it. "Simon?" she asked with an ironic tilt to her head. " I know I'm the guest but may I, er, invite you?"

Hadley walked out of the living room, already

trailing her T-shirt behind her. By the time he'd joined her Simon had an erection and the relentlessly hot shower seemed both to lash them together and to unsteady them, Simon's penis butting awkwardly between his navel and hers till she crouched down in the confined space of the shower-stall and took him in her mouth, her hands fastened on his hips.

He let go of her hair and lifting her up, embraced her. Inside the circle of his arms she rotated, the continuing shower making their skin slippery and viscous by turns, and placed her palms high up against the wet wall, her ass now towards him. Simon penetrated her vagina again and again till finally he came, clinging to her waist, his face buried in her shoulder blades. She turned again and kissed his mouth. Scarcely bothering to dry themselves, they went into the bedroom holding hands and climbed in under the duvet.

"Will I do?" she asked lightly after a pause.

"Oh I think so. I think we can say you'll definitely do."

3

They swayed and they swirled. They surged and they soared. Then they swayed and swirled, surged and soared all over again. Endlessly, it seemed. Till eventually the menfolk stood back, clapping their hands in rhythm, hitting their boot-heels in a dry staccato on the podium floor as their women took centre stage, shaking and punching tambourines, their long dark fingernails flicking free from a froth of lace cuffs, beaded bracelets and ballooning linen sleeves, and suddenly – with an aggressive tilt of the head here, a knowing gyration of the hip there – men and women alike re-formed in a circle as, to a more general clapping (the audience by now joining in), a solo violin rose on its theme from the accompanying harmonics of accordions and balalaikas. Egged on by cheers from the spectators, the fiddle rose to a frenzy of squeaks then – amid a universal roar – abruptly signalled climax, rejoining the other instruments in a basic jog-trot, its pulse and push apparently tireless...

Sarah, seated at one of the circular dinner tables, felt a headache coming on, but she also felt bad about it. If this strange Balkan music failed to excite her, wasn't this just one more proof of her dreary British provincialism? And yet wouldn't that be unfair? she wondered. Didn't she love it when Simon, as prelude to one of their afternoon trysts, put on his random compilations of Argentine love-songs and Portuguese *fado*? (True, it was other compilations – Randy Newman, Van Morrison and the like – she asked him to copy for her, but so what? Come to think of it, what had happened to those tapes? She'd lost sight of them recently.)

She had come to this gathering at the urging of Mark, who occasionally helped organise fund-raisers – in this particular case for an 'Anglo-Albanian' organisation keen to promote a new image for its homeland. To Sarah the image seemed anything but new – almost a parody of old-style Balkan entertainment, in fact – but, hell, what did she know, she asked herself. And if a few rich Brits were willing to spill disposable income in a worthy direction she for one would not cavil.

She was seated at a table set for six, although only now did the last member join them from where he'd previously stood close to the dais, clapping enthusiastically. He gave off a powerful odour of cologne and for a moment Sarah was reminded of Zac.

He grasped one of her hands in his own. It was large, with black wiry hairs running down to his finger-joints. "Welcome. Thank you for coming. I am Ervan. And you are...?"

"Sarah."

"Welcome again! You like our music, Susanne?"

"Sarah. I..."

"Excuse me." And already, as if suddenly remembering his duties, he had leaped to his feet again, was now tapping for attention on one of the crystal glasses with his heavy signet ring. The laughter and high-decibel conversation which had resumed at the other tables faltered once more.

"Ladies and gentlemen!" announced Ervan. "Welcome to this glorious event in honour of our wonderful Albania!" A scatter of applause. "This we owe to our great friend Mark! Mark, please take a bow."

At another table, Mark rose a few inches from his seat and bowed his head smilingly to the assembled, who clapped enthusiastically.

"Why are we here?" Ervan continued. "The answer

is simple, my friends — because we all love Albania!"
More applause. "We love it from the magnificent ruins
of Apollonia to those of Butrinti! From Gjirokustra to
Tirana. From — but now I stop, because where do we
not love it?"

Laughter and again more applause, now with the
odd cheer. Decidedly, thought Sarah, the man was
quite a showman. In one of Saul's movies he would
have been played in all his bulky charm by a middle-
aged Omar Sharif.

"Tonight I make no big speeches. Tonight instead
I say simply — thank you, thank you one thousand
times. With your support, with your generosity, this
wonderful evening is just the first of many. But for
now let us eat, drink and be merry... And yes, before
I forget " — he lifted his glass in a toast — "let's drink
to Albania!"

The assembled chorused back "To Albania!",
dutifully lifting their glasses as Ervan himself sat
down again and the surrounding conversations
picked up once more.

"Sarah," he said (he pronounced it with a slightly
sibilant 's' and a dark first 'a'), "you are, I believe, the
mother of Mark?"

"Correct."

"How lucky to have such an enterprising, handsome
son!"

"Indeed," said Sarah.

"But how lucky *he* is also – to have such a beautiful mother!"

Sarah merely smiled in return. Was this guy for real?

"But then – I think – you have been having these compliments all your life?"

"If I have, there's always room for more," she said.

"Tell me about yourself, Sarah! My small duties for the evening are over. I have ears only for you."

Where should she begin? And how seriously did this stranger want to know even the rudimentary details of her life?

"Well – first I was an actress, then I was a mother, then an actress again, then a producer – I ran a small pub-theatre... Hey, do you really want to know all this?"

He looked her in the eyes with alarming conviction. "Every last detail!"

When at the end she said goodbye to this most attentive and unexpected of auditors, she had the impression she had enjoyed a wonderful evening of stimulating conversation. But then again, she reflected wryly in the taxi home, wasn't that what one *always* thought when – so rarely now but, my, what a pleasure! – the entire time had been spent talking about oneself?

For the next week, Sarah was under siege. Every morning at exactly nine o'clock her doorbell rang and standing on the steps was a chauffeur – black suit, black cap, black sunglasses – holding out an extravagant bouquet. He never replied to her questions (did he indeed speak English?) merely shrugging with a smile and turning on his heel back to the dark Mercedes below. But the card attached to each bouquet said it all: *'From your pasionate admirer*!' Sarah knew only one rich 'admirer' who could misspell 'passionate'. The flowers were always roses, their colour varying from day to day. Her daughter – only fleetingly in the house these days – was vastly amused at her bewilderment; Sarah started giving them away to neighbours.

On the Saturday the chauffeur arrived with a case of Albanian wine. This time the note read: *'For my English rose some neccessary refreshment*!' Well, at least he'd spelled 'refreshment' correctly, thought Sarah.

Later that day she received a phone call. The indomitable Ervan – for it was indeed he – was inviting her to one of the most expensive restaurants in London. She couldn't find an excuse not to go.

"Sarah. You should know one thing." They were seated at a corner table out of everyone's earshot.

"You should know that I am a man of great passions. Look at me. Did you not see this from the very commencement?"

Sarah didn't know what to say. Fortunately Ervan was not the sort to wait for an answer. "I have had many women in my life," he went on. "Many many women – ah! Always they were beautiful. But now I am at an age where I seek not only beauty but also the Wisdom of Experience. What care I for silly girls without waist, without hips, but, above all, without that Wisdom of Experience?"

Sarah reflected that this man's style of wooing – if that indeed was what it was – was unique.

"Sometimes I say to myself, 'Ervan, you have had the best of it. A wife who has stayed with you'..."

"Er, where is your wife, Ervan?"

He brushed this aside as if it were an impertinence. "She is in New York, she is not relevant. I say to myself, you have a wife who has stayed with you, you have five healthy children..."

"*Five?*"

Again he swotted it away. "They too are in New York. My daughters – I fear – are becoming whores. My youngest child, my son, he has too much freedom already. He calls me a 'fat capitalist'. I say to him, 'Rather this than the fat communists of my own childhood! With *them* you would not have been too happy, my boy! Oh no!'"

"What are you saying, Ervan?"

He reached across, folding in his enormous hands one of hers. "I am saying that for these three, four weeks I am, Sarah, entirely yours."

"Excuse me? Three or four weeks?"

He shrugged massively, as if the plaything of a mightier destiny. "After Christmas I rejoin my family in New York. I resume my business interests."

"Which are...? "

Again he treated it as of no consequence. "Let us talk of more interesting things. Let us talk" – he squeezed her hand – "of my sudden love for this Woman of Experience!"

Curiously, Ervan's revelation that he was leaving in a month came to Sarah as a reassurance. It seemed this slightly crazy man was offering her a brief affair that would complicate the domestic arrangements of neither.

"You will go back to New York, you say?"

"Yes! Let us use this time to love and rejoice!"

Why not? thought Sarah. She had been half persuaded to laugh off his florid declarations as she had his relentless bouquets, but she ruefully acknowledged from her days with Saul – and his not dissimilar style of courtship – that sheer bloody persistence paid off. She likewise acknowledged that in the last few years she had slowly joined the ranks of women who, alas, no longer needed to avoid eye contact when it came to men. How many more such opportunities before the source dried up altogether? But then what about Simon? she wondered. Could she justify to herself this light-hearted adventure? With him she had at first been scared of the possible consequences, a measure perhaps of how seriously she had taken the whole business. But how quickly it had become routine! How different Simon was in his lack of passionate intensity!

"Well, Sarah?" asked Ervan, now holding both her hands in his and looking her in the eyes. "What do you say?"

Later that evening in Ervan's Mayfair flat, Sarah lay next to him on the huge double bed. She was still wondering if this wasn't a one-night stand. His enthusiasm, always slightly comic, seemed unabated after their love-making; now he stroked her thigh gently, his penis, small at its proudest, now detumescent and hiding in his enormous quantity of body-hair.

"I think my beautiful Sarah is deciding," he said softly.

"How so?" she replied with a smile.

"She is thinking, this ridiculous stranger with his passion, his devotion... 'Should I go, or should I stay?'"

"Nonsense," she lied with a small laugh. And indeed in her mind she was already moving on. Tomorrow she would go out and buy some more alluring underwear. After all there were only a few shopping days left till Christmas.

4

The building, an imposing combination of smoked glass, sandstone and steel, rose some twenty storeys from its faux-marble plaza nestled coyly behind St Paul's.

"Blimey," thought Simon. He read the scribbled address again – there was no mistake – but on entering the lobby he checked the panelled slats above a temporarily vacant desk. There it was all right. *Trumble Finances. Floor Six.*

The academic term had come to an end and Simon had promised himself he'd do this one bit of business before he slumped into seasonal sloth.

The lift gave directly onto a deeply-carpeted office space, partitioned in glass and notable for its quietness. It was peopled by youngish men in casually expensive suits and young women in pale blouses, dark skirts and heels. All sat absorbed at computer screens. Occasionally a man walked over, leaned down and in the low tones which Simon associated with churches and art galleries whispered something in the ear of a colleague, male or female, who merely nodded and continued working. Such Christmas decorations as there were seemed strangely token.

Before him at a reception desk sat two attractive young women preoccupied with mini-computers of their own. They at least had entered into the spirit of the imminent festivities by wearing paper-hats at facetious angles.

"May I help?" said one, looking up with a bright smile.

"I'm here to see Tubs, " Simon began. "I mean Thomas. Thomas Trumble."

"And you are?"

"Simon Heycock. I have an appointment for twelve."

The girl smiled again and pushed a button in front of her. Only now could Simon see a thin white tube running back from behind the woman's ear till it was lost in what was visible of her burnished, honey-coloured hair.

"A Mr Heycock for you, Thomas?... right." She looked up again. "Go right on through, Mr Heycock.

He's expecting you."

She indicated a partitioned office at the far end set against an entire wall of glass. On each side of it the London skyline was magnificently framed.

"Simon!"

Tubs had risen from his desk, and after shaking Simon's hand, he gestured towards a suite of two armchairs and sofa in deep brown leather behind which loomed a flickering TV screen and a shoulder-high fir tree festooned in tinsel and glitter.

"Drink?"

"Er... bit early for me, Tubs? But you go ahead."

"I need no encouragement," chuckled Tubs and moving to the drinks cabinet turned off the TV. As far as Simon could tell, it had been showing not FTSE readings but an old episode of *The Simpsons*. While Tubs poured himself a generous gin and tonic – "Sure you won't?" – Simon admired the view. Down below him a couple of tugboats, almost touchingly anachronistic, rocked side by side on the low tide.

"Quite a view, Tubs."

"Nothing but the best for your eminent pal!"

"Weren't you Old Street way before?"

"Indeed!" Glass in hand, Tubs spread his imperial girth across one of the armchairs, gesturing for Simon to take the Chesterfield. "Then when Pop retired, well, I moved up and in, so to speak. This was Pop's old office, in fact. Many a time just where you're sitting now sat Trumble Junior in his short trousers and blazer, quaking as Pater opened the latest school report!"

"How is your father? Still with us?"

"Only just, dear boy. Only just. Down there in West Sussex with the old lady and rather a bad case of Parkinson's."

"I'm sorry."

"So it goes. And yourself?"

Simon had a flash of his own father in his last home – institutional, with a pervasive smell of urine and Dettol. Already deep into Alzheimer's, he clutched his son's wrist with a hand whose frailty Simon would always remember, its skin so taut, so thin and so transparent he fancied that the dark blood-coloured botches beneath, shot through with magenta veins, were so many pressed flowers beneath a layer of frost...

"Dad died a couple of years back. And Mum ten years before that."

"Ah, sadly I remember. Still – we're all mortal. Cigarette?"

Simon hesitated then shook his head with a smile.

"Quite right," declared Tubs, lighting up a Rothman's. "It goes without saying this building *is* a smoke-free zone." He inhaled deeply before winking. "But then again I have special privileges. God help us when the pubs and restaurants go the same way! Now, old chap, how might I help you?"

It had always been an unlikely friendship. Who in the first week of college has not struck up a shy conversation over dinner with some inappropriate booby, scorned by one's later 'real' friends (as oneself, no doubt, is scorned by his) and only to be acknowledged thereafter with a rueful half-smile when paths cross in the middle of a courtyard, in the middle of a term, in the middle of two college careers which have known only divergence and difference? Adulterers, Simon fancied, might feel the same embarrassment when, long after their brief affair is over, they find themselves sharing the same commuter train up to town.

Tubs Trumble had come into Simon's life by the kind of fluke that can have long-term consequences; in the first year they shared the same staircase at their Cambridge college. Tubs had popped down on day three to borrow some sugar in return for a glass of sherry. "Sherry?" Simon had thought at the time. "*Sherry*? Isn't that the tipple of the already middle-aged?" Recognising immediately what very different beasts they were, he assumed that would be the end of it.

Not so. While Tubs soon enough was spending his evenings down at the Pitt Club with crapulous and extraordinarily noisy pals of Tory persuasion and while Simon found his own natural milieu among film-freaks and devotees of hard rock with a tendency to mild recreational drugs, their friendship – or at least some ironic camaraderie – continued apace. For Tubs was, in his way, a source of continuous delight and hilarity.

Two incidents would remain with Simon always. In those last prelapsarian days – single-sex colleges, all gates locked at midnight – it was not unusual for undergraduates who had stayed out later than allowed to climb in illegally over the college walls. Tubs one night managed the climb, hoisting himself up on the backs of some deeply unfortunate drinking-companions from another college, but grew scared of the drop the other side. Here he sat like Humpty Dumpty, eventually abandoned by his fair-weather peers and only spared hypothermia – so he averred – by the arrival of a college porter doing his rounds.

Caught red-handed ("Red-handed, d'you say? Red-buttocked more like! And bloody painful too!") Tubs was already no doubt up for a college fine, but he made matters worse by claiming broken glass or a spike on the top of the wall in question had "pierced the ol' wedding-tackle, don't you know" and in consequence the college – "after all, in bloody loco parentis, don't let's forget!" – had jeopardised continuation of "the mighty Trumble lineage" and would likely be sued for their irresponsibility. In the event, fearing more trouble than it was worth, the authorities preferred to forget the whole incident, though thereafter a couple of embittered porters claimed getting Tubs down from his perch had brought on severe physical debility in one case and an early retirement in the other.

Or, then again, the Senate House incident. It seemed that on a previous Long Vac back home in West Sussex Tubs had hooked himself some strapping, lantern-jawed lass name of Daphne, stalwart of the county set, and had encouraged her to motor up to Cambridge, where he would show her around and – in his words – "get her thoroughly pissed with a view to Ugandan affairs, know what I mean?" Well and good, except that by some oversight, Tubs had now invited her on the very last day of his Part Two Tripos. Never one to be tormented by indecision, Tubs knew where his priorities lay. As Simon and the rest sweated it out, row upon row, under the scorching roof of the Senate House, just a few chuckling audibly at the one exam desk left conspicuously unoccupied, a screech of tyres from the Senate forecourt announced the belated arrival of Tubs and Daphne in her Pa's snazzy second convertible. A car door slammed, and they heard the recognisable voice of Tubs declaring "Shan't be a moment, darling!" before the entire Senate House frame seemed to shake, the door opened, and Tubs pounded wheezingly up to his vacant seat.

By this time Simon and all other examinees (indeed all invigilators) had sat mesmerised. Those in front of him, turning round, could see the familiar Trumble brow – so seldom troubled by deep reflection – experience a momentary furrow. A pause, as Tubs finished flicking through the austere pages of closely-typed questions. With a breezy smile to all around him, he respectfully shuffled the exam-papers into one neat pile, patted them fondly and declared in a loud voice "Nothing for *me* here!" before pounding back to the door, jumping into Daphne's car – the engine had significantly been left turning – and bidding his paramour convey the two of them *toot sweet* to Grantchester and a favourite lunchtime watering-hole.

Somewhat to Simon's surprise, he and Tubs had continued to meet up, occasionally dropping out of each other's ken only to be realigned by a summons from Tubs to some new "nosebag" or "giggle factory" he'd found close to work and that Simon must – "absolutely *must*, dear boy!" – get to know. By this stage, Tubs had left his failed degree and family odium long behind. Wasn't he "Pop's one and only"?

Wasn't he, for all his faults, part of the "family biz" and indispensable to its continuing éclat? Well, Tubs seemed to think so, and who in the firm that bore his name would dare say otherwise? ("Curious, dear boy, that they don't entrust me with the really *juicy* accounts! But hey ho, anything for a quiet life, eh?") Stranger still was how, like Justice Shallow, he seemed to have rewritten the scenario of his college days, now remembering Simon as his "one true friend" ("not like those ghastly would-be politicos I used to hang out with"), who had ministered to him when he had a hangover and given sound advice on how to negotiate the next scrape he'd inevitably got himself into. Simon had scant memory of such good deeds but was happy enough, perhaps three times a year, to be audience to more adult scrapes, recounted by Tubs with some brio and usually involving a girl who sounded interchangeable with the legendary Daphne.

Simon's mobile rang.

"I'm so sorry, mind if I take that?"

"Of course, old chap. I'll just freshen up my glass. Sure you won't?"

It was Hadley. Simon looked up from his call. "Tell me, Tubs. Is there a wine bar near here? A pub?"

Tubs gave him a name, duly relayed by Simon before he rang off.

"One of your numerous fillies, Simon?"

"Excuse me?"

"You can't fool me. Never knew a man who kept his cards closer to his chest than you, old bean! Now, where were we?"

"It's very simple. When Dad died he left me a few thousand which have been sitting around in my savings account ever since."

"Invest, dear boy! Invest!"

"Which brings me here. Aren't you involved in that sort of thing?"

"Indeed I am. You've come to the right place."

"I'm looking for something low interest but low risk. Any ideas?"

"Why don't I call in the lovely Nathalie? She'll sort you out."

Two hours later Simon sat with Tubs in the wine bar previously recommended. Nathalie had indeed 'sorted him out' with admirable efficiency and despatch, hindered rather than helped by occasional interjections from Tubs himself, who had looked on with a proprietary air as she shuffled though a folder of options. ("Listen to this girl, Simon! Not just a beauty, eh?") Simon hadn't had the heart to point out that Nathalie's suggestions invariably ran counter to

Tubs's own – nor indeed to underline that it was her advice he'd preferred to go with at the end of their session.

The lunchtime clientele of brokers and City traders was thinning out now. They would be working right up till Christmas Eve, but already there seemed a barely-contained recklessness in the air.

Tubs looked at his watch. "Well, seems to me I should be getting back. Then again" – this with a twinkle – "Would they really miss me, I wonder? And it is nearly Christmas after all. What say we go for one last shout?"

"Actually, Tubs, I'm meeting... a friend, and then taking in a film. She should be here any time."

"All the more reason for another round!"

But even as Tubs began to heave himself from his seat Simon saw Hadley walk in. "There she is now." He waved her over.

"My! She's a corker. And – I say! – what about that piece alongside her?"

Hadley had been followed in by Breeze. Simon stood to introduce them.

"I hope you don't mind," smiled Hadley. "Breeze and I were having lunch and so..."

"Of course not," said Simon. "So were we." He gestured a little lamely at the collection of empty glasses between him and Tubs and, choosing to ignore Hadley's cocked ironic eyebrow, made the introductions. "The thing is," he continued, "We'd agreed to catch the new Minghella."

"Right," nodded Hadley.

"Catch a Minghella?" asked Tubs. "That some sort of foot disease?"

To the surprise of both Simon and Hadley, Breeze laughed uproariously.

"What will you have?" asked a gratified Tubs.

"Oh, make mine a vodka Martini. Straight up, with a double twist," said Breeze.

"That's my girl. What about you two?"

"Er... we *should* go if we're to make the 3:30," said Hadley pleasantly.

"Right," said Simon. "Breeze?"

Breeze merely leaned back in her chair. "You know, guys – I think I might just hang here and enjoy that vodka."

"The most sensible thing I've heard all day!" triumphed Tubs. Already he was en route to the bar when, struck by a thought, he turned with a stage whisper surely heard by most of the Square Mile.

"Last thought on this morning, Simon... Nathalie's terribly good and all that but – mark my words – go for Northern Rock! *They'll* never let you down!"

Simon would not hear from Tubs for some time. It

was Hadley who surprised him a week or so later with the news.

"You know your ample friend Tubs?"

"Yes. And?"

"He seems to be having a torrid affair. With Breeze."

As for Simon, so also for Hadley the academic term came to an end. She had promised her parents she would visit them back home; Breeze, as it happened, had done likewise with her parents. They shared a cab to Heathrow and caught their separate flights after much farewell hilarity about their respective 'beaux', double-dating et cetera.

After her departure and in the run-up to Christmas, Simon tried not to think of Hadley for fear of unduly sentimentalising their relationship. He did not mention her to Sarah when they spoke a couple of times over the phone, any more than Sarah mentioned Ervan, so recently departed. Each to the other sounded pleasantly preoccupied with the daily round. A suggestion that they should have a pre-Christmas drink somehow fell off the agenda as rapidly as it appeared, Sarah claiming all-consuming preparations for a dinner to which (Zac excepted) all her relatives were invited, and Simon finding it equally convenient to plead next term's lecture notes, which needed 'reworking' before he 'lost the will'. In reality, neither wanted a meeting or conversation where they'd be forced to talk about their recent *amours*.

Simon spent Christmas itself with his brother and his brother's family just outside Oxford. His two amusingly abrasive nephews – twins aged thirteen – quizzed him on his sexuality. "You're not married! You don't support Arsenal! Hey, Uncle Si, how long you been gay?"

Over in Pittsburgh Hadley suffered a parallel inquisition from her two half-sisters, both now married and with tiny kids of their own. What could she tell them, or indeed her mother, about this new relationship on which she herself had not got a proper fix?

Sarah rejoiced in the seamless transition from pampered mistress one moment (Ervan had been lavish in his attentions) to contented matriarch the next, distributing presents to her new grandchildren with particular relish.

Zac's greatest pleasure that Christmas was sitting on the floor and opening huge shiny packages from Iris, who had thoughtfully bought him more rolling-stock for his toy railway. Unfortunately it also meant he spent long hours locked away in his train room. But at least this way, sighed Iris, I can keep some sort of eye on him...

At the very beginning of the New Year, Hadley returned and Simon whisked her off to Paris. They stayed in a split-level studio apartment owned and occasionally rented out to friends by a colleague of Simon's in the Modern Languages Department. Simon wondered *en passant* if it was not, to use an egregious phrase, a 'fuck-flat', but his obliging, reserved workmate was not letting on.

Paris was a city he knew relatively well. He'd first come here on a school trip aged thirteen, and successive visits had run alongside interests which were to wax and wane with the passage of time – existentialism for one (was *any* averagely alienated teenager impervious to the consoling bleakness of *L'Etranger*?), European cinema for another (Arletti's cry "Atmosphere! Atmosphere!" would resonate down the years – or at least Simon's years).

For Hadley, who'd never been here before, it was a revelation. Back in the US, for the most part at campus film societies, she too had seen those old movies by Carné and Prévert and now for the first time she could match her celluloid memories against reality. Here on the Left Bank, in the midst of a warren of cobbled streets which still managed to cling on in the very shadow of Montparnasse's gleaming makeover, she could figure the baker's downstairs, the steam-laundry opposite and the bistro next door as appropriate backdrops to black-and-white stereotypes still there in spirit if not in the flesh – the concierge who ate tradesmen for breakfast, the daughter who paid for the sharp suits of her scar-faced boyfriend (he of the eternal *calvados* in the aforementioned bistro, he who knocked girlfriend's teeth out last year when she almost laughed at another man's joke), the Paris of canal-locks and short-haired *jolies-laides*, of Marie-Louise waking pregnant in the top-floor maid's room while two storeys down the adulterous Dupont, notary and freemason, slept an untroubled *grasse matinée* which would prove his last ("Marie-Louise has fainted while floor-polishing!" "Marie-Louise has confided all to Madame!").

No. Paris, she found, was sleeker, shinier and altogether more hip these days, but Hadley reflected that its buzz and energy had merely found new forms. Still men stared at you in ways unsettling for those used to more Anglo-Saxon restraint. Still couples seemed to make out behind the steamed-up windows of bars and brasseries. Still the pervasive sweetness of Gitanes set the blood tingling in a city which – EU dictates notwithstanding – would never wholeheartedly commit to the notion of the 'smoke-free zone'. Even Simon, it seemed, had capitulated, now regularly filching her cigarettes.

They spent the days checking out galleries, bookshops, funky *prêt-à-porter* (Simon, somewhat meanly she thought, had outlawed visits to the Eiffel Tower and the more hackneyed tourist-spots), evenings in bars and restaurants which even now, so far from Spring, dared to spill out on to the pavement and stayed thronged till a time of night, or rather early morning, that struck Hadley as a fuck-you Mediterranean reproach to the likes of, say, London's Oxford Street, already deserted and mournful from midnight on.

One afternoon they went to a cinema near Saint-Michel. It seemed to Hadley that a number of Parisian cinemas were happy to programme those old much-loved films which in New York and London would only be seen on TV or in rare museum showings. They went, at Simon's nostalgia-fuelled suggestion, to see *Jules et Jim* by François Truffaut, a film Hadley had seen on television aged sixteen and had remembered as delightful but nothing more. Now this movie, with the free-spirited Catherine loving two men and beloved of both, blew her away. Was it the case that certain films, like certain books, waited till you were old enough before pouncing again like 'the beast in the jungle'? This time, as not before, she could appreciate its technical fluidity, its freedom from a more theatrical scene-by-scene dramaturgy. But much, much more important to her were other kinds of freedom implicit here: a combination of the light-hearted and the tragic, of (how else could she put it?) the Permissive and the Innocent, except this took no account of just how unjudgemental and uncensorious it all was. There was sadness here to be sure:

"You said to me: I love you.
I told you: Wait
I was going to say: Take me
You said: Go away."

Yet in this old black-and-white movie she found a suggestion that one could still love to the full without being merged or absorbed in the other, that for reasons more spiritual than carnal one man wasn't necessarily enough. This movie about how to love, how to live, seemed to be saying that an exclusive passion could block out a curiosity for the world, that a choice meant loss.

Hadley and Simon made love at night and again on waking. They made love sometimes in the mid-afternoon, a prolonged and boozy lunch beforehand usually aiding. Somehow to Hadley this seemed the best time of all – consonant with what she recognised to be a no doubt stereotyped reading of Parisian *moeurs*.

For his part, spending so much time with Hadley —
a time in which they saw none but themselves and
were forced further in on each other by the unfamiliar
environment — Simon was not altogether surprised
when his subconscious sought other company, other
associations. He dreamed of Julie... Julie and Hadley.
What was the connection? he wondered. Only this
perhaps — and here, did he but know it, he was moving
in the opposite direction from Hadley — that great
passion was, like great bereavement, a narrowing of
focus, an unpeopling of the world.

His unconscious had at any rate got there before
him because, having not dreamed of Julie for so long,
he now found her again not here in Paris but — of
all unreal, dream-like places — in Venice, a city he
knew far less well. She was dressed in jeans and a
long tapering black coat and led him from the basilica
of St Mark's, laced with marble foam and sculptured
spray, down shuttered passages which were somehow
at the same time the book vaults of his old university
library but were now dream-padded and swollen with
shadows. On she went, rarely looking back, across
small bridges over high black water and on down
apparent culs de sac, each with its shoulder-high
shimmer of light reflected from the canal below, until
they reached a massive iron door, the stone steps to
which were constantly under siege from the ebb and

flow of the tide. Magically, they were next the other side of it, crossing from a vine-strewn cloister to where some kind of birdbath was held aloft by a marble Pan, then up a flight of stone steps to another door, this time half of sweating wood and half of leaded glass. Now she led him through vast, high-ceilinged rooms shrouded in darkness to a panelled hallway lined with mirrors of all shapes and sizes in frames gilded and austere, some as sombre as the canals they had crossed. Others were so freckled with stains that Simon felt he was looking at his own image in a pond across which had drifted dead leaf-fragments or delicate seaweed.

Julie stopped before one such mirror, concave of surface. She turned and smiled at him kindly. The glass behind her seemed to gather to a point inside itself all the angles of this shadowy, panelled room as if, like some starch-stiff tablecloth, it needed just one twitch of the wrist and the entire room, walls, ceiling and floor but also Julie herself (now lifting a hand in what might be a farewell but then again might be a blessing), would stream headlong to the mirror's lustrous centre, swallowed up and never to be seen again.

Which was exactly what happened. Simon stared at a mirror which now reflected only himself. He turned. Where *was* Julie? He turned again, beginning to panic.

He was alone, desperately alone. He awoke that night in a sweat, sitting bolt upright, only to rediscover in a flood of relief Hadley sleeping next to him. Yes, perhaps that was it. In mourning or in the intensity of this, his new passion, he found himself moving into a mental space where the Significant Other occupied all his thoughts and the rest of humanity in past or present form could just disappear. He would no more seek to explain to friends (or indeed to himself) what he was now experiencing with Hadley than he had sought to articulate his emotions at Julie's death. What could they understand or contribute who were not already, so to speak, within the charmed Circle of Knowledge? And none but he knew the curve and contours of the particular circle that was his own. Simon had respect for what he had heard of bereavement therapy, for its beneficial effects on individuals so smitten, but it had seemed as irrelevant at the time as it would be now to seek out some confidante, some Horatio figure, and bore them with his obsession. Yet, far from being a burden, this new all-absorbing preoccupation of his – hey, why not give it a name and call it Love? – seemed like some lucky treasure-trove which he would remember on awakening each morning and return to in his thoughts throughout the day, a miser chuckling as every few hours he turned back to gloat over his hoard.

They left Paris and came back to London, content during the journey to say little and with a deeper sense of intimacy than before. Had they been told, neither of them would have believed that their happiness together was running out of momentum as surely as the Eurostar pulling into Waterloo Station.

5

Hadley arrived promptly at 5:30. On the first floor of a nondescript building just off Islington's Upper Street she found a big well-lit room with four large desk-spaces and walls lined with posters advertising previous productions by Zac's company. Two people were hunched over computers. Hadley announced herself to one of these, an efficient-seeming woman of about forty who looked up with a smile.

"I'm here to see Zac?"

"Right. I'll tell him. You are...?"

Hadley gave her name and was invited to take a seat while the woman went to a door flanked by two windows at the other end of the room. She knocked softly, poked her head inside and reappeared almost instantly.

"He'll be with you in a minute. Would you like a coffee?"

Hadley declined and the woman went back to her computer. The other office worker, a youngish man with a shaved head, looked up only once to nod at her then continue as before.

Another term, another assignment. Hadley would have been happy to move the *Streetwise* presentation sideways to her enthusiastic friend Breeze, but – perhaps maliciously – the Prof was having none of it. She had duly phoned Zac's office and booked an interview. Now temporarily left to her own devices, Hadley took stock. It was only the framed posters, some flyers for various productions and a couple of battered sets of *Spotlight* that would have indicated to the innocent that this company dealt in theatre as opposed to, say, marketing or computer software.

A moment later Zac emerged from his sanctum, wearing a dark T-shirt, cargoes and trainers. As he came towards her, smiling pleasantly, Hadley realised that in the crowded reception room of the wrap-party she had not registered his gait, which she would best characterise as a kind of challenging saunter – the torso tilted fractionally backwards with the arms held a little way from the hips and swinging ever so slightly. Where, she asked herself, had she seen that walk before? She found the answer almost immediately. Of course – Frank Sinatra and Norman Mailer, as glimpsed in documentary TV footage back home.

"Hi. Come on in," he beckoned, and she noticed in addition to the gait an involuntary compulsive gesture, the thumb of his left hand forever stroking the underside of an embossed ring he wore on his little finger. His den seemed no less spartan than the outer office: a desk and two chairs, a phone and laptop, a banquette by the wall and more framed posters. He gestured for her to sit down opposite him.

"Tina offered you some coffee?"

"I'm fine, thanks."

"Then – Hadley – remind me what I can do for you."

When she'd explained her course assignment, Zac nodded routinely. "And so?"

"And so I thought we might talk about the way you get actors to turn dialogue into, like, *performance*?"

Again he nodded, as if he'd been half-expecting this. As well he might, thought Hadley, already pulling a notebook from her shoulder-bag. For while preparing for this interview she had come to learn that this was the legendary kernel of Zac's work, perhaps more important even than his workshopping of plays on the back of actors' research. 'Actioning' he called it, and indeed finding the action behind the word, the transitive verb behind the supposedly throwaway line of dialogue was, Zac maintained, as important to drama as it was to life in general. *"I say this and by so doing hope to seduce you." "I say this and intend thereby to humiliate you."* That he had adapted this technique, stolen it even, from Stanislavski was beside the point. He had made it his own. It energised everything he directed and without it, he maintained, words could only fall in the spaces between the characters up on stage like so many dropped tennis balls.

Less well-known to the public at large – and not at all to Hadley at this point – was how Zac employed this his trademark procedure to ends more personal once outside the rehearsal room. Suggestion. Manipulation. Even, at times, a certain suave bullying. The gradations varied according to the situation, but few were the women who did not at some time feel the heat banked up behind an apparently neutral statement. It was a short step from statement to proposition, and if seventy per cent of women so addressed walked away, well, thirty per cent stayed on or came back after going through stages of first outrage, then amusement, and finally gratification at having so drawn the attentions of this showbiz luminary.

Almost an hour passed before Hadley laid down her pen, smiling as she massaged her aching wrist.

"Is the interview now finished?" Zac asked with an ironic tilt of the head.

"I guess," she replied. "Thank you."

Zac stood and glanced through to the outer office. His PA and production manager had gone off for the evening, leaving only empty polystyrene cups and yellow Post-Its stuck to the frames of their computers. With a brisk clatter Zac lowered the Venetian blinds and turned.

"To business, then."

Hadley blinked. "Excuse me?"

"I thought you might like to suck my cock."

Hadley kept a fixed smile. "I'm sorry?"

"You heard."

With a grin Zac unzipped his cargoes and pulled down the front of his briefs. No boxer shorts for him, thought Hadley, with what she had long recognised was a maddening tendency to fasten in situations of tension on the most irrelevant and banal of incidentals. No foreskin either, she further recognised, as Zac cradled his still semi-soft penis in his right hand, almost offering it to her like a gift. What was *that* all about? she wondered. Hadn't she been led to believe that among Brits only Jewish guys were 'cut'?

"I don't think so," she smiled. She walked towards the door, sidestepping Zac, who was still holding on to grin and penis alike. "Perhaps some other time?"

To her surprise, Zach merely nodded and, zipping up his trousers, shrugged philosophically. "Well — you've got my number."

"Hell yes, " said Hadley. "I've got your number all right."

Mark finished lunch with Sarah at the Camden Brasserie and insisted on paying the bill. This New Year *tête-à-tête* was at his prompting. He wanted reassurance that his mother had enough money to cover her expenses and — now an additional headache replacing school-fees — college bills for Sophie.

These days Mark had two small kids and a wife of his own to support, but hey, he was flushed with the success of his last film, the 'Euro rom com' *A Week In Rome*. It had put in only a so-so performance at the box office but was doing very nicely on DVD sales & rental. Could it be that some frivolously entertaining movies were like chocolates — guilty secrets better consumed in the privacy of one's own home? Whatever. He was more than ever ready to help out now Zac was no longer on the scene. And for the first time in twenty years or more, he could have Sarah entirely to himself.

If Mark was honest, he'd acknowledge that he hated Zac and had done so ever since the director and his mother had got together. As a small boy living with Sarah in the big house left them by Saul, Mark had grown accustomed to her disappearances of an evening, the nights she stayed out altogether leaving him in the care of their live-in nanny, the unexplained bouts of tearfulness or euphoria he sensed were obscurely connected with these comings and goings. Sometimes he had woken up in the middle of the night and, making his way to the huge fridge in the basement kitchen for a glass of milk, would pass her bedroom door knowing instinctively she was not there – only to find her next morning sitting on the living room sofa (or in summer in the garden) reading a novel and looking up cheerfully to bid him good morning and ask what he wanted for breakfast. It had been a companionable co-existence, though shadowed by his father's death and rendered more poignant by the knowledge that for his mother as for him, each memory was losing its definition and colour as rapidly as the video-taped movies he had begun to watch obsessively: the enormous white boat in a sparkling blue sea, bicycle rides through the leaf-canopied backroads of southern France and chaotic, hilarious ski-trips to Klosters, in all cases with staff attendant to their every caprice.

Mark was a clever boy. All his teachers said so. But, progressive as his posh independent day-school was, they also felt bound to point out that he paid little attention in classes. Later Mark would come to interpret their criticism as resentment at what they knew to be his future life – a life made easy by a trust fund he would one day enjoy in full and, meanwhile, a mother who denied him nothing except her undivided attention.

When the thieving started, it coincided with the arrival of Zac. First minor treasures belonging to schoolmates (a geometry set here, a kaleidoscope there), then articles from local newsagents and toyshops. It culminated late one afternoon in his being seized by an irate shopkeeper who, keeping a brutally tight grasp on his hand – Mark's shorter legs could barely keep up – frogmarched him back to his appalled mother. Apprised of his misdeeds, almost speechless with shock and remorse as they stood there on the high stone steps of the front porch, Sarah had tearfully promised the man that there would be no more trouble if the shopkeeper agreed to take the matter no further. Once inside the darkened, cool house more tears and recriminations had followed: did Mark not have everything a boy could possibly want? These things he had stolen, he had only to ask – would she not have bought them for him? Mark played the one card he knew would always win: his ability to make his mother feel guilty at her inadequacies, real or imagined, as a parent.

New to this relationship as to all family commitments, Zac said little to Mark directly about these events, being content to sit loyally at Sarah's side and nod in agreement to whatever she said, occasionally clasping her hand when she seemed once again on the point of tears. Slowly, Mark came to loathe this man whose presence now prevented him from his earlier breakfast conferences with his mother, their shared intimacies, the sense he had always enjoyed of The Two Of Them Against The World. Now Mark found her bedroom closed for other reasons and himself only allowed to jump on her bed, creating amiable havoc, when Zac had left for work or was off in his study – a room newly converted for that purpose and to which Mark was never allowed access. Occasionally he would bump into Zac wandering absent-mindedly through the house with no clothes on and, retreating quickly, would be both fascinated and appalled by the glimpse he had had of the man's grisly grown-up genitals. Was it somehow by association with this that he now found a private nickname for his stepfather – the Worm?

The thieving began again, but now on a larger scale – department-stores, large West End bookshops. His headmaster had no option; Mark was expelled from his school and re-consigned by Sarah to another equally expensive institution where uniforms were not necessary, where the other kids too seemed the offspring of media luminaries but where attendance and any hint of aberrant behaviour, especially concerning drugs, were rigorously monitored. Academic standards were high and, somewhat to his own surprise as well as that of his mother, Mark performed outstandingly in GCSEs and A/S levels without ever seeming to study or indeed focus attention on anything except his now vast collection of movies, favourites among which were the glorious epics his father had produced at the peak of his career.

Mark smoked now (though his mother disapproved she kept quiet, imagining worse temptations in the path of a rich young adolescent), and leaving school with no wish to pursue a university career he soon became a familiar sight, cigarette rakishly fixed in a corner of his mouth, on film-sets where he worked as a runner. In early days these were movies by directors whom his father had brought on, directors who, loyal to Saul's memory, were happy to indulge in a little mild nepotism. But soon Mark was perceived as quick, resourceful and trustworthy, and he advanced rapidly to the role of First Assistant. It would only be certain second-rank actors and extras who would remember long afterwards his tendency to bully when out of the sight of the director, his fits of blazing anger which subsided almost as rapidly as they appeared, and in general a quite extraordinary emotional volatility which could also take the form of great, spontaneous generosity. Also emerging now, and apparently from nowhere (though his mother put it down to some middle European gene inherited from his father), was a facility for languages which served him well in dealing with international casts and crews. It came as no surprise therefore when one day Mark announced he'd had enough of pandering to the dreams of others: from now on he would forge his own path in the world of European co-production.

Mark eventually moved out of his mother's house, but his animosity towards Zac continued unabated. The Worm went from strength to strength as a theatre director; even Mark, occasionally yielding under protest to his mother's plea that he attend with her such and such a press-night or preview, was bound to acknowledge their outstanding quality – all the more so in that Zac consistently chose new material without the safety-net of tried-and-tested authorship, material which (if one didn't know better, scowled Mark to himself) one would fancy had emanated from a radical, albeit slightly puritanical, artist of unimpeachable integrity. "Trust the tale, not the teller", Mark's English teachers had always told him, but since the earliest days of Zac's presence he'd got a whiff of the man's sexual adventurism and would never forgive the hurt thus done to his mother.

Somehow circumstances contrived only to increase this animosity. Coming into his office one day – Mark had started to rent a suite for his company in the newly fashionable area of Hoxton – he found his recently-appointed PA Angela poring over a copy of *Spotlight*. They were working on a smallish independent project, an art-house co-production with the French, set in the theatre world of the Belle Epoque. The original director had fallen through, but with the moneys secure they had carried on casting.

"Idea for the director!" announced Angela, looking up. "Someone suggested Zac Slocombe." She had no idea that her new boss was indirectly related to Zac.

Mark merely tilted his head in polite interest. "Does he do film?"

"No," she conceded. "But he's done the odd television. And God knows he'd be a natural for those rehearsal scenes." (The script centred on the difficult rise to stardom of a young actress in the era of Sarah Bernhardt.)

"Well, it's a thought, I guess," said Mark, again

giving little sign of his true feelings.

Now Angela nodded at the copy of *Spotlight* open in front of them. "And guess what, all these three were in Zac Slocombe's production of *Streetwise*." By an accident of the alphabet, the headshots of three actresses – all considered to be promising and all in their late twenties – were displayed on the same double-page. "We could cast Rachel, her sister and Flore in one fell swoop."

"Remind me," nodded Mark. "*Streetwise*. When was that? Five years ago?"

"Eight years to be precise." They had been joined by Mark's production manager, Dave, now discarding his motorbike leathers as he grinned at the page. "I was an ASM on that production – er, you might have a problem, particularly if you hire all three. Then again perhaps not!" He seemed to be enjoying a private joke.

"You mean they're a tad too old?" asked Angela.

"No," said Dave. "Zac slept with all three of them during rehearsals. Although to my knowledge, not all at the same time."

Angela laughed heartily and Mark did his best to join in before turning back to his own partitioned room. He closed the door slowly and stood trying to fix a date in his mind. Eight years ago? Wasn't that when his mother had 'accidentally' or otherwise taken

an overdose? Later she'd said it was all a mistake –
a misjudged combination of valium and pain-killers
taken for a swollen tooth. Mark had been more upset
at the time than he cared to show; Sophie was only
nine or so and ever present, ears pricked for the
slightest hint of discord.

Mark suddenly gasped and swore forcibly.
Without realising it, he had crushed in his hand the
polystyrene cup he'd been holding for the last ten
minutes. The dregs of his coffee had splashed across
hands, shirt and shoes.

" Work with The Worm? I think not, " he said to
himself, and turned to find a box of tissues.

If this last year or so had been pleasantly Zac-
free, Mark knew all the same he hadn't seen the last
of him. Now, as he stood by Camden Lock bidding
farewell to his mother, he could at least reassure
himself that the Worm was maintaining payments
towards Sophie's education.

The weather had turned very cold, but here the
pavements and roadways alike were submerged
beneath a continuous stream of youths, drug-dealers,
street-touts and tourists – Sarah remembered
Zac once referring to this raffish ambience as
'Bartholomew Fair' – and the sunlight was so bright
the two of them had resorted to sunglasses. Sarah

made Mark laugh by suggesting that the combination of shades and overcoats left them looking like well-heeled gangsters.

"So you're all right, Ma? No problems?" He gave her a last kiss on the cheek.

"Ah! There's always problems!" she laughed. "It's called growing old."

"Come now..."

"Thank you for the lunch, Mark."

"I'll call."

Mark disappeared with a wave of the hand and Sarah was left to forge a path home among more street-traders, more tourists. She realised she had not been fibbing – there were no problems to speak of – but likewise, with Ervan now gone, there were no peaks of exhilaration either. Could she just pick up again with Simon as before? Did she want to? Did she dare?

Hadley was pissed off – and, to make matters worse, pissed off with herself. Why couldn't she just wipe the memory of Zac's outrageous offer? This, after all, was a girl who while growing up in American cities had been flashed a number of times; speedily crossing the road or getting to the other end of the subway platform, she'd as often as not ended up laughing at the pitiful behaviour of these men. So what was it about the encounter with Zac which continued, maddeningly, to buzz in her brain? God knows, neither his looks nor his personality was overwhelming and at first she'd wondered if it weren't some delayed adolescent gratification at being thus propositioned by a celebrity director. If so, she had all the more reason to be annoyed with herself. But on reflection she decided otherwise, remembering an apparently unrelated incident back in the US.

She had been appearing in a classy TV series – in truth her part was minimal – of the kind which ran for years at a time but intermittently imported a star to swell the ranks of the regular cast (who had meanwhile become stars in their own right, thanks to the series' popularity). One particular star thus inducted was an actress now in her seventh decade and semi-retired. She had taken a shine to Hadley, perhaps seeing in the younger woman some echo of her earlier self. (Fat chance, thought Hadley. The star, who had had several husbands and was rumoured to be immensely rich, had married a Hollywood legend, long since dead, when she was at least ten years younger than Hadley was now.) At the older woman's suggestion and to Hadley's delight they ended up sharing a trailer on set, as a result of which Hadley enjoyed six weeks of uncensored access to the star's memories, gossip and extravagant mood-swings. If she alone on the set was spared the vitriolic force of the diva's tantrums, Hadley – somewhat as expected – spent much of the time fetching and carrying as a *de facto* assistant, helping her to learn her lines while fielding phone calls from agents and intimates alike. Then and afterwards she would always say this bumpy ride was worth it.

One day 'Franzee' (as she was known to all but the general public) revealed that a well-known journalist had submitted a request to profile her for a glossy upmarket review. An in-depth interview, a photo by Annie Leibovitz. As Franzee put it with characteristic saltiness, "the whole fuckin' enchilada, baby."

"So what's the problem?" Hadley had asked.

"The problem, sweet pea, is that this particular journalist is a louse. A low-life."

"How so?"

"He can write okay, so I guess from a certain point of view he deserves his fame. He also deserves to have those no doubt inflated balls of his twisted off and fried on the nearest barbecue. Before he does the same to his next interviewee – in this case yours truly."

"I still don't get it."

"Demolition jobs, baby, one and all. Nine times out of ten he cosies up to you, swears he's your lifelong friend for however many meetings it takes, then puts the knife in when it comes to writing the article.

Believe me, he's done it to two, three of my best friends back in LA."

"Then tell him to go fuck himself up the ass," shrugged Hadley, somewhat contaminated these days by Franzee's idiomatic profanity.

"Right," Franzee had cackled. "Maybe I'll just do that."

But, strangely, Hadley had felt no real conviction behind this last remark and it subsequently transpired that Franzee had said 'Yes' to the interview after all. When this at last came out — by then Hadley was back in the Village — it was quite as devastating as anything she could have imagined or Franzee could have predicted.

The 'in-depth interview' took the form of unguarded, supposedly off-the-record gossip scrupulously transcribed for the world at large. Franzee's occasionally malicious but usually good-hearted asides were magicked into the sustained and sneering philippic of an embittered old crone at least twenty years past her sell-by date who'd lucked into celebrity merely by association with her first, legendary husband and had continued to berate the world ever since for not taking her seriously as an actress in her own right.

Hadley read the interview, her hands almost shaking. Why oh why had Franzee agreed to do it?

She didn't need the money, and Hadley believed her when she'd said she did not nowadays covet publicity or media attention.

Hadley could only think of it as some Dark Appointment With Destiny on Franzee's part, some crazy wish to stare down her demons and settle what forever after would have remained Unfinished Business. And who knows, she might have told herself, it could yet turn out all right, I might yet come up smiling at the end of it.

Well, if that was the intention, Franzee had spectacularly miscalculated. She had indeed been skewered and roasted, ridiculed and vilified for the benefit of a gloating public. And if Hadley had been so shaken, how in God's name had she, the subject of the interview, reacted back home in Hollywood? Her 'best friend'-cum-slave for those six weeks would never know, not seeing Franzee again, nor be surprised that this should be the case.

But now, in what were at first glance entirely different circumstances, Hadley found herself comparing what she thought of as her 'Zac encounter' with Franzee's. Unfinished Business. An Appointment Evaded. Some dark confrontation which she could easily forego but which she'd always remember as precisely that – an evasion. Was it merely that she was flattered? she asked herself again. How could that be when she'd learned from Breeze and others that the man was a serial romancer, a 'sexual terrorist', as another gossip had rather melodramatically put it, and she herself would just be the next link in an endless chain?

Breeze, she knew, would have reacted differently – boasting far and wide of the offer before backing off – but then Breeze was only half her intimate and confidante; some part of Hadley recognised a reality more intense, more unyielding in the private encounters of the self than Breeze would ever care to know, and for this reason if no other she had kept the whole episode to herself.

For Christ's sake, she wanted to protest (but protest to whom?) that she didn't even fancy the guy, finding something – as the Brits would have it – slightly 'creepy' in his heavy eyelids, that tight mean mouth and his 'up-for-it' gait. So why now was she giving herself such a hard time?

And then, finally, there was Simon – Sweet Simon, as she thought of him. Was their liaison really a relationship? If so, was she effectively closing it down before it had even begun? But this also had its problems. She'd sensed either that he was involved with someone else and not talking about it or – perhaps worse – that he was that particular kind of diffident Englishman who, never less than charming, could as well 'do without' in the down-and-dirty world of sex and real feelings, the kind who, loathing confrontation, would shrug and mutely move on, albeit offering to include her in an unspoken roll-call of ironically affectionate ex-girlfriends who would occasionally return for a 'fuck-buddie' night but knew they were ultimately onto a losing game when it came to this eternal escapee from the world of commitment. In this perspective Simon seemed rather less 'sweet' – a man whose unemphatic amiability masked at best an eternal hedging of bets and at worst an indifference, an emotional survival strategy hardened into selfishness.

Hadley sat taking stock in the rather cheerless bedroom she rented, one of three in a house shared with fellow-students. On her shelves were two kinds of book, indicators of where she'd come from intellectually and where she still might go should she eventually undertake a full doctorate. On the one hand, *The Second Sex, The Female Eunuch, The Feminine Mystique*. On the other, *The Empty Space, From Text To Stage, Dreams and Deconstruction, Freeing The Natural Voice*. She had lived with these books off and on for years – they were an unchanging comfort zone – but now somehow the titles alone seemed to invite a new itinerary. Was she forever to stay in her own Empty Space, this side of Dreams, the Voice (natural or otherwise) Unfreed?

Without further reflection she picked up the phone and dialled the number of Zac's office. To her consternation, it was Zac himself who picked up.

"It's Hadley — I've been thinking about, well, all manner of things."

"And?"

"Perhaps we might meet after all? This week even?"

"Of course," Zac replied. "What about — say — Thursday? The bar of the Dorchester Hotel? Eight o'clock?"

"Fine."

"Thursday then," said Zac. "I look forward to it. I've been thinking about you too."

Hadley hung up and wondered what on earth she had done.

6

Zac stood at his desk, shutting down his computer for the night. If Hadley wanted to see him again, he surmised, it could be for only one reason. *She* might tell herself it was with a view to further negotiation, some principled establishment of ground-rules along the lines of 'You don't expect me to just fuck you like that, do you? We need to talk about this – *if* I'm really up for it, that is.' And so on and so forth. But long experience had taught Zac that a return call like Hadley's meant the woman in question always *was* 'up for it' – she simply didn't want in Zac's eyes (and perhaps more importantly her own) to seem a Slag, Push-over or Pinhead with no volitional compass of her own.

As Zac saw it this was all par for the course, no

more than a kind of self-protective mating-dance −
better yet, a Theatre of Seduction where the Action
was screaming loud and clear ("*Yes, I accept your
offer*") the subtext manifest ("*But I have my pride,
you know! My self-respect!*") and the end ("*Did you
bring a condom?*") as inevitable as the duel scene or
marriage at the end of a five-act drama. His part in
it all was to be solemnly attentive to each necessary
cue ("*Of course you have self-respect!*"), shoot back the
further lines expected of him ("*If you didn't, could I
in turn have respect for you?*") and keep a straight
face while covertly checking that, yes, he had indeed
− in just such an eventuality now become a foregone
conclusion − transferred the new packet of condoms
to his present pair of trousers when he'd put them on
that morning. For Christ's sake, thought Zac, in the
States, as far as he could ascertain, it was practically
inscribed in the rituals of 'dating' that only on the
third encounter was it acceptable for the woman to
nod and take the petitioning lover to bed! Iris had
been different − *she'd* accepted straight off − and at
the time Zac had been left to consider whether he
was entirely pleased. Did this not bespeak a certain
desperation? Then again her enthusiasm *had* been
flattering...

' Ho-hum. Zac scraped with his thumb the inner
side of his ring. A song from his parents' generation

came into his head, as it often did on occasions such as these.

> *As time came around, she came my way*
> *As time came around, she came...*

Zac's parents – his father a psychoanalyst of some distinction and his mother an interesting if not altogether successful novelist – had had a fondness for the clever lyrics of Lorenz Hart, Ira Gershwin and Cole Porter, notwithstanding their 'serious' involvement with a local string quartet (his mother playing cello, his father violin). His mother used laughingly to recite whole lines at a time – Zac remembered with particular relish:

When love congeals
It has the faint aroma of performing seals ...

or, more expansively,

With love to lead the way I've seen more clouds of grey
Than any Russian play
Can guarantee...

And when one evening, no less laughingly, she had tossed off an unattributed quotation about the 'potency of cheap music', the young Zac could scarcely suspect that the theatre luminary so referenced (Noel Coward) was just one among many theatre luminaries he would come to know well, if only through their texts.

He had gone on to study at Trinity College, Dublin, and there for the first time had encountered, again through their texts, luminaries by the barrel-load. In Restoration Theatre for a start: particularly appealing to Zac for its camouflaging of sexual predatoriness (Zac was already gaining a reputation among fellow students as a 'bed-swerver') beneath rituals of codified behaviour and turns of phrase as elegant as they were cynically purposeful. Here he had started to direct, his artistic talent and his opportunities for carnal conquest growing apace with pleasing symmetry. He started to specialise in new work, for there engagement with the writers became direct and full-on, plus it was one more arena in which a certain manipulativeness, always part of his character, could find fruition. Thus emerged a dualism which would characterise his life from the moment when, ultimately, he was to turn professional back in England: a tendency to work with actresses and female writers in a very genuine wish to promote women, their vision, their voice, in an epoch when they were crucially marginalised in British theatre, and at the same time a wish to fuck these same women as often and in as great a number as their beauty and charm might provoke and they might allow.

With his first major professional engagement he had struck lucky – directorially if not, as it happened, sexually. He had neither chosen nor indeed been offered a new play, but had settled instead for the revival of a work by the much-neglected Restoration writer Aphra Behn. (Subsequently, and in no small part thanks to this production, she would be rediscovered and championed by feminist academics.) Hitherto Zac's successes in student theatre had been almost accidental, a matter perhaps more of flair than of substance. They were performing in Nottingham, and one evening early on in the rehearsals for *The Rover* he had been offered a lift back to his digs by an elderly actress; Zac had yet to find the income which would fund a whole series of smart, usually rather racy cars. On the way back the actress, called Thea, had remained resolutely non-committal about how he, the fresh-faced tyro, was faring in a rehearsal room where he was so evidently less experienced, less professionally equipped than anyone else. Seeking approval and reassurance – no, *her* he did not wish to fuck! – he had fished for compliments, but Thea had maintained her polite reserve till, both irritated and disappointed, Zac had finally expostulated: "Of course. I'll expect you to tell me where I'm going wrong. *If* I'm going wrong."

They had reached the outside of Zac's rather grotty digs. Thea turned off the ignition and sat for a moment looking out through the windscreen. At last, as if she'd come to a decision, she put on the handbrake and swivelled slightly towards him.

"I *could* tell you," she said pleasantly, "that you're doing a marvellous job. That we the actors all love you, which is true enough even though you perhaps don't deserve it. I could tell you that when the reviews come in – *if*, that is, they have such a thing as reviews in this benighted place" – she gestured grandly to the provincial terraced street stretching ahead of them – "that they will probably say how an inventive young director has 'coaxed' – that's their favourite word – '*coaxed*' fresh and appealing performances from a thoroughly drilled and orchestrated cast packed with seasoned professionals." She paused a fraction. "For which, read: tired old hacks saved at the eleventh hour by whizz-kid from Cambridge."

"Trinity Dublin, actually."

Thea waved the objection away. "There'll be a certain truth in all this. Some of us *are* tired old hacks." She named a couple of the more elderly actors in the cast who seemed less interested in Zac's rehearsal procedures than in rolling their own cigarettes while they read the racing results in the local evening paper. "I myself will probably be described as 'luminous'. I've been 'luminous' for quite some years now."

She paused to smile ruefully at the thought, and Zac chose the moment to intervene. "Do I take it this is not how you see the production?"

She barked her slightly patrician laugh. "Of course not. Though – as I say – you will probably get away with it, as you will the next show and the show after that. But then, one day, sooner or later..."

Another pause as she turned once more to look into the far distance of the street. Zac by now had retreated into an offended silence, awaiting only the first polite moment to be out of the car and away from this ghastly old Cassandra.

"My dear boy." Thea had turned towards him once more. "Permit me to call you a 'boy', but you are so, next to most of us in this production. My dear boy, although Hector and Bevis" – she was referring to the two elderly actors already mentioned – "are tired old hacks, although they are lazy and sometimes mean-minded, they are content to go through the motions of rehearsing, of following your suggestions because they find you quite sweet. We all find you quite sweet. But come the night, they will deliver their average-to-good performances as if you'd never been there in the first place."

"So what in God's name am I doing wrong?" protested Zac, more forcefully than he'd intended.

"You really want to know?"

"I really want to know."

With another pause, another nod of the head as of some further decision just taken, Thea asked, "Have you got your notebook with you?"

Zac drew from his book-bag a small pad in black moleskin. It would be the first in a long line which he'd keep thereafter in a special drawer, a new notebook for each production. One day – though of course even Zac could not envisage this – they would be seen as a precious 'archive' to which theatre academics would request access.

"Let's start with the problem of Generalisation."

"Pardon me?"

"Generalisation," she repeated. "It's the enemy of all Art, and particularly of acting. That is, if like me you consider acting an Art?"

Zac nodded.

"What is Hector really *saying* when he delivers – with some deftness, this much even I would admit – that first speech of his?"

"Well, I suppose he's saying that he..." Zac dried, suddenly finding the – to him – obvious thrust of the speech somehow, well, *too* obvious.

"Yes?"

"I don't know. You tell *me*."

And Thea did tell Zac. As she told him in the next half hour, parked in what he would always remember as that crummy street with its fish-and-chip shop at one end, its betting shop at the other and in between houses like his digs, two-up-two-down, sometimes divided into flats and sometimes not, the entire story of this their play, not now as an excuse for a rather jolly, swashbuckling romp with lots of pratfalls, extravagant tirades and actory *tours de force* but as a series of challenges, negotiations and confrontations.

Thea would talk in that thirty minutes of how each scene had for its characters an Objective and how that Objective was part of a Super-Objective realised – or not – by the end of the play. She would talk of how each main character – she left none out – should identify a very clear trajectory as well as more pragmatic adjustments along the way which might or might not affect that trajectory. She would talk of how no line of dialogue is 'clean' of intention or effect, how one line delivered properly can then resituate the next, this in turn resituating the one after; she referred to it as a kind of perpetual 'chronometric adjustment' like a peripatetic compass which could constantly reset itself as it crossed a varying terrain.

Now Zac had caught echoes of this in his reading at college and after; he recognised, for example, the voice of Stanislavski behind Thea's description of the Objective and Super-Objective. But – and this was crucial for him at this time as ever after – he had never known such elusive principles to be pinned so precisely to a text he was staging. It was as if that pinning left the play with a secret structure all its own – a pattern, a design, one might say, if that were not misleadingly suggestive of mere decoration – which, on turning the play-carpet over, one could follow with one's finger as precisely as explorers followed a route-map across some known but vexatiously wayward desert, a desert where, sure, one could just trudge on and no doubt, exhausted, embittered, make it to the other side, but at a terrible price to the soul and the energies and having taken no real cognisance of just how rich and compelling was the landscape.

Thea finished her lecture and paused before turning away. "Then again," she said smiling, "it might all be crap." She gestured for Zac to be gone, out of the car, back to his digs, where in the event he would stay up half the night 'plotting', in for himself a new sense of the word, the gradients and contours of a play-landscape, now revealed anew by a penetrating and, yes, beautiful starlight.

Zac spoke very little to Thea for the rest of the rehearsals and almost not at all during the run (in any case he was largely absent, already hustling for more work down in London). But from time to time when she was not in a scene, he fancied he caught a glance from her – a glance, well, he could not say either of affection or approval exactly, but of a secret communication transmitted and now picked up, a kind of intellectual seeding which both of them recognised, before in her case returning with a small private smile to her embroidery or the *Times* crossword.

After that, Zac turned his show around. It was, by any standards, very good and – thanks be to Thea, thought Zac – a hundred times better than he had originally deserved. Even Hector and Bevis seemed to find something in their performances to surprise and delight with. After the run was over and the cast scattered, Zac would see Thea perhaps no more than two or three times, occasions when she seemed to only half remember him. Later he heard she'd had a stroke and retired from the business altogether. But by then Zac had encountered his other great influence – this time another director, some twenty years his senior.

Guy Taunton had a slightly maverick reputation in British theatre. Overwhelmed as a young man in the 1950s by a visit to London of the Berliner Ensemble, he had done more than most to introduce Brecht to the English, gaining something akin to veneration in his profession, though no great renown outside of it.

Even among colleagues he was considered 'difficult', 'unclubbable', his great shyness interpreted as curt bad manners (no "Darlings, you were wonderful!" from *him*).

He was also gay, but very privately so, never allowing his personal life to declare itself in the often camp badinage of the Green Room. What he saw in Zac was, perhaps, a similar tendency to keep his private life – however extravagant – close to his chest while exercising with almost puritan rigour the fundamentals of his art. And if Zach rarely touched on Brecht, or indeed anything outside the English canon (Chekhov would prove a major exception), he, like Guy, suggested a certain austerity and seriousness far removed from showbiz flannel. Above all, perhaps, a clarity both in approach and final performance which commanded respect.

Well, Guy had died, but not before bringing Zac on board for certain productions which his failing health was no longer equal to – provocative new writing, the odd more difficult Jacobean play.

Zac had gone to visit him in the Royal Free as he lay dying.

"Guy?"

"Ah. Zac. Is that you? How very nice. Please forgive my embarrassing... *appareil*." He gestured weakly to the tubes and drip-feeds which had been keeping him alive. "Come to ease my passage?"

"I hope so, Guy."

"You know, when I was at school – a very long time ago now – I played John of Gaunt in *Richard II*. You remember Gaunt? Fulminating as he lay on his deathbed against the state of things, against England?"

Zac nodded.

"What in Christ's name was the old cunt on about?"

Zac smiled tightly: the 'c-word', as it had come to be known among liberal circles, was something which only Guy's generation and class allowed themselves without embarrassment in a late twentieth century dominated by political correctness.

"Of course," continued Guy, " I know – we all do – where it falls vis-à-vis Richard, the squandering of a national heritage and all that stuff... But now I wonder – forgive me, I've had time enough for such wondering in this place" – again he gestured to the machinery around him, the room, the hospital at large – "Now I wonder if it's not a metaphor for the body itself – his body in the event – overrun and devastated, put to torch and sword by the armies of the night. Call those armies Old Age. Call them Cancer."

Again he gestured weakly, though this time indicating his own body. Zac, still maintaining his fixed smile of interest and sympathy, wondered where all this was leading. But already Guy seemed to have switched tracks.

"Still got that pretty wife of yours?"

Zac nodded again. It seemed neither the time nor the place to elaborate on the continuing difficulties of his marriage to Sarah. And besides (was it the morphine?), Guy had immediately jumped tracks yet again.

"Since I've been here I've asked myself the same question time after time. What's it to be? The satisfactions of the Life – or the satisfactions of the Art? And *should* they be at odds with each other? God knows, Trevor seems to have managed well enough..." He was referring to an eminently successful director who had, it appeared, combined familial contentment with a professional versatility that took in serious new work, Broadway musicals and esteemed productions of the classics.

"I'm sorry, Guy, I'm not quite with you?"

"The likes of you and me. Do we surrender all to what we might laughingly call our Art, forever staying within the cloister? Or do we recognise that we are only whores in the marketplace, out for what we can get? Isn't there some way we can *genuinely* combine the two? (Forgive my pomposity – but when if not on his deathbed is a man allowed to be pompous?) Isn't there some way in which we can be at one and the same time honest *and* gratified? Wise *and* successful? Isn't there some way in which we can blend and merge both the doing good *and* the doing well?"

Zac had walked away with tears in his eyes, still disentangling the drug-fuelled ruminations of Guy in his last hours. And indeed, his last hours they had proved to be. Guy died later that night, and Zac felt he had lost a second father.

As for the 'merging', Zac had since then only half lived up to his mentor's strict code. He had stayed true to their concept of Art, never wavering when it came to the most honest and strenuous application of his skills. (Sometimes he dreamed of a knighthood – but what the hell?) It was in a different area that he felt he could not follow Guy's high principles. He wanted women's bodies. He wanted – what was the phrase? – to be 'gratified' in the flesh and in the triumph of that flesh.

All of which brought him back to this newly-arranged rendezvous. Zac, the Divided Self, opened his desk-diary and checked his schedules for the week ahead. On the one hand a quite punishing agenda of rehearsals, meetings with his set-designer, a preliminary consultation with the marketing people. On the other an evening of seduction and 'nookie'.

Hey – who except Guy, he wondered, would

seriously argue that the monk and the hedonist in Man could not inhabit the same body?

In another part of London – and, as it seemed to him, without warning – Simon suddenly found that Hadley was gone, leaving him with only a renewed taste for cigarettes. He could no more account for her disappearance than he could for a slight but unmistakeable shift in the London weather. Several times he tried her number – always the voice-mail – and text messages and emails proved similarly ineffective. Had he offended her in some way? If so, how? Had she suddenly gone back to the States for a while? Then why not tell him? He momentarily considered locating her through the Tubs-Breeze connection, but never having shared the secrets of his love-life with anyone, it seemed a little foolish to start now, however bereft he felt, however stricken. He had no option but to continue doggedly with his work.

In his class they had moved on from the late Victorians and Simon permitted himself what he called a 'proleptic glance'. ("What's 'proleptic'?" asked Annette, the attractive American always to be found in the front row. "Er...like when you hit a later chapter on your DVD menu?" ventured Simon. "Then why not say so?" muttered a usually silent malcontent further back.) He alluded briefly to Modernism and fragmentation, how the solipsistic voice could one day become a cry in the wilderness which might in turn become stones in the pocket, helping the despairing author to drown herself.

"But Virginia Woolf and Bloomsbury, well, that's for another time, perhaps another course. Let us return, meanwhile, to the century's end..."

In his eye-line Annette had loyally inscribed 'proleptic' in her notepad, though even at this distance and upside down Simon could see she'd misspelt it. For fear he might appear to be pondering her generous cleavage, he turned away.

Iris was prone to paranoia. It came in waves. Just when she thought something was fixed, inescapably within her control, it slipped sideways and she was left to fumble and fret.

Witness Zac, whom she thought she had pinned down. She'd made it clear. Finished the wife! Finished his legendary philandering! She'd have none of this shuttling between the new flat he'd allegedly bought with her in mind and his old home back with Sarah! And yet there always remained this doubt when he slid off to another rehearsal or 'meeting'. Might it not be to another assignation or sly tryst?

Or, then again, her career as a playwright. Her first, then her second, play had been shaped and championed by Zac himself – to the exasperation (so she had reason to believe) of many whom he worked with who doubted that this no doubt pretty Irish actress had any real talent at all as a writer. Well, she would show them!

She had met Zac in Dublin, when he was over from London directing workshops for the Gate Theatre. She had sat mesmerised as he talked to actors – herself included – about scenes from an O'Casey play, emphasising the characters' through-line and 'objective'. When he had chatted her up in the bar afterwards, he had expressed an interest in seeing her work-in-progress and she had believed him when later he said that walking away from their meeting was like walking away from Paradise. The next time they met he had been effusive about the manuscript he'd received in the interim ("Some work to be done here, but very promising!") and to his suggestion that they should now go to bed together she had agreed at once. Why not? Despite the husband back in Dalkey. Despite Zac's reputation. He said he was crazy for her, that she was a fine writer – she'd have been a fool to refuse. After all, wasn't this man responsible for bringing on some of the most singular talents in the last twenty years? Who would seriously dare to gainsay this extraordinary imprimatur?

It had all been so different before they met. Iris

remembered a childhood before the Celtic Tiger had shown its claws, before EU subsidy and general affluence had briefly made her homeland the most expensive country in Europe. Now she remembered her favourite walk before and after she'd got married. It was the coast road from Dun Laoghaire harbour with its view across the strand to Sandy Cove: a few paint-chipped rowing-boats, that vaguely Art Deco house in white at the foot of the Martello tower, the elderly pink gentlemen skinny-dipping off Forty-Foot. Now even this treasured part of her past was just one more stretch in the extended theme-park known as the New Ireland. Hadn't even Dalkey itself, *her* Dalkey, once no more than a little village-town cringing in Dublin's shadow, become the home to millionaire pop singers and American film stars?

At least for the present, thanks to her association with Zac, she too was a player, more likely to stop over at Dublin's swanky Shelbourne or visit upwardly mobile friends in their converted lofts near Liberties than trace old paths that reminded her of her native poor-cousin status. Well and good. But that left evenings when her saviour and new partner was mysteriously absent. Today was no exception. Rehearsals would have ended. His office telephone was not answering. Where *was* Zac? Sometimes she fancied she'd like to tie him to a chair and keep him there all his days.

7

They walked towards his parked car.

"What the fuck was that all about?"

"Oh come on, Zac. It was really kind of interesting."

"Interesting like root-canal work is interesting? Like shingles is interesting?"

"No. Like *Vertigo* is interesting. *Vertigo* without the MacGuffin."

"Excuse me? Who's MacGuffin?"

Sometimes Hadley despaired of Zac. Here was one of the most adventurous theatre directors in the UK but whenever in their short acquaintance she had exposed him to something off his beaten Anglo-American track – in this case an early-evening NFT screening of *L'Immortelle* by Alain Robbe-Grillet – he fretted and whined like a small boy. Indeed at times,

Hadley fancied he was the American and she the European.

"Are you kidding?" she asked. "Next you'll be telling me you've never heard of *Vertigo* either."

"Oh I know that all right. These days I know it every time I get to the first landing."

Hadley laughed obligingly, but she was aware of a certain edge to his voice. And, yes, the man now ushering her into his posh English car was thirty years her senior, a man who'd kept himself in pretty good shape, but 'immortal'? Certainly not. Still finding her bearings in this new relationship, Hadley had scarcely allowed herself to think, let alone fantasise, about the future. What would life be like if they carried on together till she was, say, fifty and he eighty? As it was, her sisters back home, getting wind of this affair and the age-difference, had amused themselves – and if truth be told, Hadley also – by referring to him as the Amorous Arthritic, the Geriatric Giovanni.

"Next you'll be telling me you haven't heard of Robbe-Grillet. Or Godard. Or Artaud."

"Who's Artaud?" he said – with, however, a twinkle in his eye. And putting the car into gear, they shot off.

It was all part of a jokey deal, rather sweet at this early stage between them: she would introduce him to something new and he would do likewise for her. He had warned her that his 'surprise' would entail a couple of hours' driving, and as he clipped a computer print-out of directions to the dashboard (how she hated these faux-walnut surfaces!) Hadley was content to lean back and listen to his tapes of Ry Cooder, Van Morrison and Randy Newman, being only intermittently startled from her reveries when, expressing admiration for some particular track, he revealed that he was less familiar with who was singing than she was.

Zac powered the car through the suburbs and onto the motorway. They arrived at what was clearly their destination – just outside Warrington, Zac informed her, a town in the North West of no great cultural importance. Then why, wondered Hadley, did he seem to be tense with a scarcely suppressed excitement? The well-heeled suburbs through which they drove were, it seemed to her, like many another with their expensive detached houses, double garages and crescent-shaped driveways.

Zac checked his print-out and drove through one particular gateway. A few Chinese lanterns studded the patio (the 'deck' as Hadley thought it), illuminating a path down into an extensive garden. There some guests were lingering, cocktails in hand, around a pond into which gurgled a stone conduit – what would turn out on closer inspection to be a gargoyle, open-mouthed, its eyes wide with horror.

As Zac parked his car at the end of a line flanking one side of the garden, Hadley finally realised what this was all about. She felt slightly fearful. But, hey, when had the new, the exciting, not been tinged with some kind of apprehension?

Zac, turning towards her, seemed to read her thoughts. He squeezed her hand. "*Et in Arcadia ego*?" he smiled. Then – "Er – what's the first person plural of ego?"

"Ego recognises no plural," she shot back, rather pleased at what under pressure passed for wit.

But if Zac heard, he made no comment. Before she knew it they were out of the car, he had grasped her hand affectionately and they were within range of the half-open front door – heavy black lacquer, some wind-chimes just visible, Marvin Gaye playing inside – by the light of which a dark-haired woman of about forty stood wearing only bikini briefs, high heels and a calf-length negligée. Her breasts stood out in a strangely conical way, thought Hadley, as she, evidently the hostess, offered them two ready-prepared glasses of white wine.

"Welcome. And you are?"

"Zac and partner. I emailed."

"Of course. Welcome again. You've, er, been to this sort of thing before?"

Zac nodded, relieving her of the glasses and handing one to Hadley.

"Then you know how it works," she smiled. "That'll be fifty pounds."

With his free hand Zac found the notes in the back pocket of his cargoes. Smoothly and with smile still in place, the woman folded the bank-notes and they seemed magically to disappear somewhere about her person. (Where? wondered Hadley.) She gestured to what they could now see were French windows round to one side of the house and open to another part of the garden; from within came the sound of laughter and clinked glasses. They stepped sideways across the patio, through the ballooning light curtains and – as Hadley conceived it – into Babylon...

So this, she thought, is what they called a 'swing party'. She had heard about them in New York but had never got this far. In some respects it seemed like any other social gathering – except the men here, for the most part early middle-aged, were wearing nothing but towels round their waists and the women, aged anything from twenty to sixty ("Oh those sagging breasts", sighed Hadley to herself) were dressed, or rather undressed, much like the hostess – in heels and panties, plus in one case an unbuttoned blouse. Drinks in hand, mingling amiably beneath the tastefully-lit reproductions of Renoir and Modigliani, these couples were conversing as if they were fully clothed, and at this stage at least it was indeed still as couples they presented themselves, the only apparent singleton being a strikingly well-built black man. Was it his physical splendour, wondered Hadley, that had led the hostess to bend the rules and allow him in unaccompanied? It was clear from an anecdote he was telling that he was an accountant; the amused circle listening included, it seemed, a bank manager and his wife.

Now some of them paused in mid-conversation to smile at Hadley and Zac as they made their way past to a corridor above which hung a computer-generated sign reading 'Cloakroom'. At its dark end were two doors, these marked in similar style 'Caballeros' and 'Señoras'. Here Zac turned and hugged her briefly – "One minute, okay?" – before disappearing.

In the darkened 'Señoras' changing room, Hadley registered racks of hangers draped with dresses, two-piece suits and brassières. "Oh my" she said out loud, only to be aware of a thin young woman sitting in a corner armchair, entirely naked but for panties, her arms crossed protectively across her chest.

"Just arrived?" asked the woman.

"Uh-huh."

"I don't know what I think about all this," said the

woman, her face still in shadow. "It's my husband's idea. He's absolutely determined."

"Right," breathed Hadley.

"You a virgin too?" asked the woman.

"Excuse me?"

"I mean, a virgin to... this kind of thing?"

"Yeah. Guess I am."

Suddenly Hadley realised the woman had started to sob. "Hey..."

"'S all right," said the woman, now breathing heavily. "Who knows?" she continued, attempting a slight laugh. "Perhaps I'll enjoy myself."

Hadley turned away, taking off her jeans and jacket and leaving on only her shoes, panties and waist-length linen shirt. She checked herself in a full-length mirror on the wall. Yes, unbuttoned – that would seem to be what's required. Meanwhile, the woman in the corner seemed to have recovered and now rose from the chair.

"Mind if we go out together?"

"Sure," said Hadley and, herself leading, they emerged from the room into the semi-lit corridor.

Zac was waiting, dressed in only a towel and a T-shirt which declared in bold capitals 'THEATRE DIRECTOR'. He took Hadley's hand as the other woman glided past with a somewhat frozen smile. "You okay?"

Hadley nodded, allowing him to lead her to the first door on the right, which turned out to be a brightly-lit kitchen. Once again, it could have been almost any party except for the white-towelled men, mostly bare-chested, and the women wearing nothing but heels, underwear and, sometimes, a blouse.

There were some six guests there and now a man and woman stepped forward to greet them, both in their mid-forties, the man wearing only a sarong and his partner no clothes at all except for a pair of heeled leopard-skin mules. Hadley found it difficult to keep her eyes averted from the woman's breasts and cropped pubis.

"Hi. I'm Thelma," said the woman.

"And I'm Stewart," said the man.

"Some wine?" asked Thelma, and Zac nodded for the both of them.

As his partner turned to the fridge and retrieved a bottle of Sauvignon, Stewart leaned somewhat over Hadley. "And what do *you* do, if I may ask?"

"She's an actress," said Zac before Hadley had time to respond. (Thanks for nothing, Zac! she thought with a flash of pique. For 'actress' read Bimbo. Read Adjunct of self-proclaimed Theatre Director.)

"Ah. Like my wife!" said Stewart.

"Is that so?"

"Sure," said Stewart with a grin. "Queen of our

local Am-Dram. You should have seen her in *Abigail's Party*! Wow!"

Thelma had returned, offering Zac and Hadley full glasses. "Pay no attention," she said. "He's prejudiced." She looked Zac in the eyes, then at his T-shirt. "Something tells me you're a theatre director."

"No flies on you," said Zac, sipping his drink.

"Would I have seen any of your work?"

"Maybe," he shrugged. "You ever get to London?"

Stewart meanwhile had ascertained that Hadley was American (how bored she was by this invariable prologue to any and all conversation!) and unashamedly looked her up and down. It seemed to her that his very chest-hair bristled with anticipation. "Here's a good joke – a joke you'll appreciate in your profession," he began.

"'Zac'? It is Zac?" asked Thelma meanwhile.

"Of course, you will tell me if you've heard it before?" said Stewart.

"Of course," obliged Hadley.

"So tell me about your directing, Zac. Is this full-time?"

Zac took it like a gentleman. "I'd say so, Thelma, yes."

"What kind of plays do you direct? Do you like Mike Leigh? I love Mike Leigh. Alan Bennett too. Hey. Come over here, there's more room..."

As Zac and Thelma moved to a side of the kitchen which had its own exit back into the living room and the rest of the house, Stewart continued. "There's this guy dies and goes up to Heaven, right? Or rather the Pearly Gates in front of Heaven where – lo and behold – Peter stands with a clipboard, deciding who should go in, who should be sent to the other place et cetera. Lots of queues, lots of people waiting for the big interview. Okay so far? Not going too fast for you?"

"Just about managing, thank you, Stewart," said Hadley, straight-faced. But if she was fearful of seeming too spikily ironic, she need not have worried. Irony, it seemed, was beyond Stewart's register this evening, and he continued enthusiastically.

"Okay – so ahead of our guy are two others, waiting like him. It comes to the turn of the first one to step up and Peter checks his name on the clipboard and nods. 'See you died earlier today. Welcome. We need to get some sense of the life you've led. Would you care to tell us how much you've been earning in an average year?' 'Three hundred thou,' shoots back this first guy, rather pleased with himself. Peter whistles slightly with admiration, makes a note on his clipboard and nodding to one particular queue already half-formed says, 'Right. Company Chief Executive. Can you join that line over there?' Still okay, Hadley?"

Stewart permitted himself a squeeze of Hadley's

elbow. As he bent forward to do so, she saw over his shoulder Thelma lightly stroking Zac's arm and leaning in to whisper something in his ear.

"Still okay, thank you, Stewart."

"Good! Excellent! So the next man in line steps up and Peter says again, 'Welcome. How much did you earn last year?' Man pauses, thinks, finally says, 'It must be around fifty thousand?' Peter nods. 'Mm. Not bad. Not bad at all. Marketing. PR. Please join that queue over there.'"

Because of Stewart she now had only a restricted view, but it seemed to Hadley that Thelma had reached out a hand and was gently stroking the area of Zac's towel that covered his crotch.

"At last our man steps up," concluded Stewart with a grin. "Peter says: 'Welcome. And how much did you earn last year?' After some thought man replies: 'Nine thousand, three hundred and twenty-six pounds.' Peter looks up from his clipboard, pauses, and says: 'Would I have seen you in anything?'"

Stewart began to laugh uproariously at his own joke, even repeating the punch-line – "*Would I have seen you in anything*?'!" – and then stepped forward to caress the front of Hadley's panties. She instinctively recoiled a pace, then, feeling mean, tried to make it look as if she'd merely shifted her body-weight from one leg to the other.

"Very good," she smiled dutifully. "Very good joke."

"So. You wanna fuck?"

Hadley smiled again. "Stewart — it *is* Stewart? Mind if I take a rain-check on that?"

Stewart's grin faded. "Er. Sure. Your prerogative. Absolutely."

But now as Hadley turned away, Zac and Thelma were no longer to be seen. Indeed, the kitchen had suddenly, magically, emptied of all other guests too. "Mm. Did you see where Zac went?"

"Aha!" laughed Stewart, slightly narrowing his eyes as if this were a conspiracy. "Cherchez la femme! Cherchez la femme!"

Hadley smiled again and briefly stroking Stewart's arm (hell, she thought, he'd taken rejection graciously enough), stepped through and into the living room. Still no Zac. Instead were three couples, completely naked, fucking on — respectively — the sofa, a leather armchair and that part of the Persian carpet which was not taken up by an expensive glass coffee-table. In all cases the couples were heterosexual and in two cases the men were on top — the exception being the armchair, where the man lay back, legs splayed, while his partner (her back to Hadley) bounced up and down on his penis. Their faces were hidden from her, and for a moment Hadley thought this might be Zac and Thelma, but a backward smile at her from the woman concerned proved otherwise. So where was he?

Already another man had stepped forward. He was still, perhaps, in his thirties, and naked except for the semi-obligatory towel.

"Can I help you? You look lost."

"I was looking for my partner," said Hadley, reluctantly admiring how this guy – unlike Stewart before him – clearly worked out.

"Ah. The Soft Swing!"

"Pardon me?"

The man smiled. "Soft Swing. You come with your partner, you fuck with your partner."

"I see."

"Then again, you could take a walk on the wild side? You and me together?"

"Sounds nice," smiled Hadley. Shit, where was Zac? "A little later perhaps?"

"Of course," said the man and with a gallant sweep of his hand allowed Hadley to pass through.

Now she found herself in a second hallway, richly carpeted and discreetly lit from above the pelmet. The first door off it was ajar. Just inside Hadley found herself almost brushing against a tall man in his forties, hitherto unseen, who had clearly been watching something. He was completely naked and had a large erection. He turned his smiling gaze on Hadley.

"Why don't you join us?"

Hadley shrugged and entered. On a kingsize double bed were two women and a man, all naked. The man lay on his back, but his face was lost to view beneath the thighs of one of the women, who now raised her eyebrows pleasantly at Hadley as if to say "The things we do for pleasure...". Meanwhile in the lower half of his body he was being pleasured by the other woman, who was alternately caressing and sucking both his erect penis and his scrotum.

The man who had invited her in seemed content merely to stand and watch. It was the woman astride the man's face who now said to Hadley, "If you like we can make room for you too?"

"Later perhaps," said Hadley, and backed out, continuing down the hallway. In the next room along – here too the door was ajar – a naked man and woman lay on another huge bed. The man's face was covered by a mask of moulded black rubber which vaguely reminded Hadley of the muzzle head-cage worn by Hannibal Lecter in *The Silence Of The Lambs*. A thin diamanté chain attached it to the man's penis, which was held erect between the luridly-painted fingernails of the woman. Now, Hadley saw, the chain was deliberately too short: each time the man tried to lean his head back on the pillows he yanked on his penis, which was then consolingly stroked and licked by his partner.

Hadley backed out. The next room along was no less tastefully lit, with the same rich carpeting as the hallway. Only a wide chair, vaguely Louis XIV, occupied this space. It was covered in a rose satin-like material. Hadley, not sure what she was thinking or feeling about this entire experience, sat down and kicked off her shoes, involuntarily spreading her legs.

She looked up. Unheard by her, the hostess who had first greeted her and Zac on the patio had entered the door-frame and stood smiling down at her. At some point in the evening the woman had jettisoned her bikini briefs and now stood only in her heels and semi-negligée. Nice bush, thought Hadley.

"Done the tour?" asked the woman with a smile.

Hadley shrugged. "Not sure. How many rooms you got?"

"Oh. This is a big house. My husband and I" – she paused – "you've met my husband?"

"I don't think so."

"My husband and I insisted on a house with many rooms. Many... opportunities."

"Uh-huh."

"Hey," said the woman, now advancing into the room and sitting down cross-legged at Hadley's feet. "I'd like to lick you out. Any objections?"

Hadley paused only a moment – "No objections" –

and allowed the woman to pull down her panties for her, leaving them to curl round one of her ankles.

The woman laughed slightly. "How nice – for a change – not to worry about premature ejaculation. Or himself not getting it up. How nice – for a change – not to worry about cocks and latex and all that jazz!"

She smiled once more, bent forward and buried her face in Hadley's waiting vagina. Hadley, for her part, leaned her head back, closed her eyes and pulled tightly on the dark mass of hair now caught between her thighs, forcing the woman's tongue closer within her...

She came almost at once.

It was two o'clock in the morning. Zac and Hadley sat in the Bentley. Now the house up at the end of the drive was strangely quiet, though the Chinese lanterns were still lit and Leonard Cohen continued to play softly somewhere inside.

"You okay?" asked Zac. "You had a good time?"

Hadley nodded and, smiling, placed a hand on Zac's crotch, soft beneath his cargoes. "Quite a party," she ventured.

Zac leaned over and kissed her briefly on the mouth before turning back to switch on the ignition. "Welcome to my world," he said cheerfully and, putting the car into reverse, began carefully to back out of the driveway.

There'd be other evenings like this, sometimes Zac staying beside Hadley, sometimes the two of them fucking separately, sometimes with others there and themselves as participants or mere onlookers according to their mood. Once he took her to an expensive flat in the Barbican, where they sat with others watching a man – apparently a merchant banker – on his knees sucking a row of cocks. Once they went to a kind of warehouse – Hadley was reminded of a New York loft – where almost everyone except herself and Zac wore some piece of rubber, on their faces or round their genitals or both. The space had 'oil-murals' – shifting globules of light – which made Hadley sometimes think of '60s rock-concerts she'd seen on film, sometimes, more disconcertingly, of medical-educational films illustrating how spermatozoa fertilised ovaries.

All in all, and to Hadley's surprise, it was a happy time, this joint adventure during which in some episodes they lost each other, found each other, lost and found each other all over again, only to end up back in bed in London (where was Zac's partner on such occasions? conveniently away for the night or the week) where Zac never omitted to recount in detail whom he had fucked and how, encouraging Hadley to do the same. Well well, she thought, it's a kind of honesty.

But for Hadley the strangest realisation was that at such parties the women, for once, seemed to hold more power than the men. They could stimulate or deflect attention and, should any male come on too forceful or too crowding, a kind of unspoken sense of community – upheld no less by the men than by the women – meant the female so harassed had only to turn on her heel and walk away, leaving the offender swiftly marginalised but, hey, accepted or not by the next woman he hit upon. Sometimes – more often than Hadley could have possibly imagined – the women initiated the coupling, leading the lucky man by the hand off to some pre-selected room or space. Hadley had never seen so much naked flesh nor so much unjudgemental recognition that the Body Beautiful was for fairy-tales or porn movies, that skin and muscle were prone to slackening and decay but – dude! Did it really matter? Who among us was immune? Wasn't it better to celebrate these surprise offerings, these unexpected gifts of the Here and Now?

And, no less surprisingly, Hadley found in the course of all this that her feeling for Zac – she hesitated to call it 'love' – grew rather than diminished, a bonding like that of children who have discovered and pooled some illicit vice previously considered unique to each and hence undisclosable. Now between the two of them they could disclose all (*"I'll show you mine if you show me yours"*) – and, so Hadley judged, Zac could exercise and articulate that compulsion to transgress in matters sexual, that need to be irresponsible, outrageous, totally 'incorrect' from any politico-moral point of view whilst sincerely holding progressive, even altruistic beliefs in the wider everyday world.

As for Zac and the women he had, well, there was no doubting it: it was her ass he loved above all others and regardless of where their coupling took place. In his favourite pre- and post-coital position he would mould his chest, abdomen and thighs round her buttocks, then pull back slightly and go on to explore her vagina and her anus – at first with his finger, sometimes (this demanded greater readjustment) with his tongue, before closing in again with his prick.

The first occasion on which he penetrated her anally she had gasped, whispered a cautionary muffled "Oh..." into the pillow beneath her mouth while with one hand she clutched the bed-frame for support. He had withdrawn, but then, sensing no real resistance, re-entered her. Hadley felt something so fundamental she could compare it only to tectonic plates shifting inside her.

He had come and lay locked, her body resettling around him.

"My turn."

"Excuse me?" asked Zac.

Messily, she disengaged herself and found within her grasp her open shoulder-bag with its pink plastic vibrator. "Now your turn." How easy it was, with just a flick of the thumb, to set this cool little engine into humming life! "You ready?" she asked with a smile. She squirmed around further.

"No," Zac replied emphatically, edging away so his prick, already softening, flopped leakily on the creased sheet between them.

"Dude! Fair's fair."

"No, I said!" And now Zac held her wrist, her hand and the throbbing piece of technology a tight arm's length away from him. "Not my thing. Forget it."

Hadley did not insist but as some kind of punishment deflected his mouth when it closed on hers. Well well, she thought, this, her 'backdoor man', remained in some private part of his body and mind a virgin who would not be violated.

And then, finally, there was the heartbeat...

Given his need to be back home with Iris, it was rare that they spent a whole night together. But on one particular evening they had gone neither to a hotel nor to Hadley's lodgings, rather to a grand house in a quiet North London crescent. Zac had no sooner driven the Bentley up into the drive than Hadley knew what it was about.

"This is Sarah's house, right?"

"Right. Does that bother you?"

Hadley shook her head, only too aware that this also was a transgressive rite, a sort of 'dare'. "And where is Sarah?"

"Where indeed? Off fucking her boyfriend, I shouldn't wonder. Though – never fear – in Italy."

"And your daughter?"

"In Norfolk. On holiday with her aunt and uncle. This way."

He led her beneath an overhanging, slightly skewed Japanese tree and up some stone steps flanked on either side by huge urns holding ferns and sea-grass. Not even a cat was stirring and as Zac slowly turned three locks in the heavy door Hadley felt the house might more appropriately be located in Provence.

Once inside, the quiet and darkness seemed even more pronounced. Zac turned on the hall-light and flipped off an alarm that had just started to vibrate. He nodded upstairs.

"First on the right. Be there in just a sec."

As Zac flicked perfunctorily through a pile of post on the front-door mat, Hadley climbed a flight of stairs and entered the main bedroom. Wow. What a bedroom it was. A veritable four-poster and, opposite, a French armoire which was surely authentic, but of what Hadley could not say.

It was later that night, Zac curled spoonlike against her, that she felt for the first time Zac's heart beating against her shoulder blades in what seemed a distinctly odd rhythm. Instead of the customary *chukka-boom, chukka-boom, chukka-boom* she'd known from previous lovers this seemed to go *chukka – BAM – boom, chukka – BAM – boom, chukka – BAM – boom* ... and then stop for an unconscionable number of seconds before resuming again.

She turned. "Hey, babe. What's with the heartbeat?"

"You've only just noticed?" Hadley tried to sense his expression in the dark as, possibly smiling, he continued: "Forget it. I've had it since birth. Call it my Distinguished Thing."

Did Zac know the Distinguished Thing was a phrase for Death itself? Hadley asked neither then nor at any time later and when, subsequently, she registered again the idiosyncratic heartbeat, she merely allowed him to hug her closer.

8

If Simon remained hurt and mystified at Hadley's disappearance from his life, he did not know that in a more poignant form he was suffering the same withdrawal symptoms experienced by Sarah now Ervan too had disappeared. When they met up again, never having made so much as a mention of the respective liaisons which had briefly enthralled them, they proved equal in their return to zero. The waters had resettled, it seemed, without a ripple of disturbance. Quite simply, and with an equanimity Simon had to admire, Sarah rang him up and smoothed all surfaces by asking him if he'd like to spend a couple of days with her in Dorset.

"Why Dorset?" Simon asked.

"Because I love it so."

"Yes, but why *Dorset*?"

"Because I used to go there with Zac. In our early days."

Was there something new in the very candour with which she said this? As if, starting again so to speak, they acknowledged not only their baggage from a former life but that now the first long period of their own relationship was part of that baggage too?

"You're on," said Simon warmly. "Next week is Reading Week."

"Perfect."

Reading Week was university parlance for half-term, and in another part of London Breeze entertained Tubs with her historico-social gloss on this, explaining with very little by way of hard evidence that back in the mists of time it was an excuse for elderly gay academics to take favoured students off in groups to Switzerland, Cornwall or Wales so that they could all go hiking in the daytime, read poetry together of an evening and then engage in relentless sodomy once the hostel lights were out for the night.

Perhaps improbably in the eyes of their friends, theirs was a relationship – maybe the only one – to survive robustly into not only a new year but better weather.

Breeze had informed Tubs of some split between

Hadley and Simon about which she knew no details, Hadley having gone 'very quiet and, like, private'. Tubs had tut-tutted, expressing sympathy for both estranged partners. As for the two of them, they found unfailing amusement in how marvellously ill-suited they were in the eyes of the world and indeed each other, Tubs finding Breeze pretty, irrepressibly good-humoured and astonishingly *American*, Breeze finding Tubs so British it wasn't true but in ways she found irresistible – his Falstaffian largeness both of body and spirit, his preppy effervescence, his libertarian generosity which no doubt included Tory prejudices Breeze wished not to explore but also what she could only describe as A Relish For Life. If nothing else, thought Breeze, he didn't have a stick up his ass like so many other Brits and if he wasn't exactly a look-alike for Brad Pitt, well, he knew how to enjoy himself and how to share that enjoyment.

It was Tubs who next got in touch, asking – nay entreating – for what he termed an urgent 'pow-wow'. Poor bugger, thought Simon. Had he been dumped as well?

"What will it be, old man?"
"What are *you* drinking, Tubs?"
"G and T. "
"Then make mine the same."

"Splendid. Ice and lime? "

It was rare for Simon to be invited to Tubs's own Highgate home. Only twice in the whole time they'd known each other had they met here as opposed to a City wine bar. As Tubs broke out some ice cubes in the kitchen, Simon admired tastefully-lit reproductions of Sickert, Bonnard and Matisse. It was all family money. Like his father's office suite these too had come down to what Tubs called 'The Only Begotten' as soon as the parents had left London for retirement.

Tubs returned with the drinks. "In your eye, old son."

"Cheers."

There was a passing moment of embarrassment, Simon aware that, like most men of their generation and class, they preferred not to talk about their 'love lives'.

Tubs cleared his throat. "Er... none of my business, old man, but I heard things weren't altogether top-hole between you and Hadley?"

"You could say that."

"Oh well. Here's hoping..."

"Thank you."

"But that's not exactly why I asked you here."

"It's not?"

"Thing is, old man, I always look to you as a source of wisdom and good judgement," said Tubs, looking up with what could only be described as a shy *moue*.

"Tubs. P-lease. I couldn't judge my way out of a paper bag."

"Untrue! Untrue! Remember that time you saved my bacon over that – er – mild *débâcle* in the JCR?"

As it happened, Simon did remember the incident. In their third year of college, he had been involved in a student production of a play by Ionesco. Returning one evening after rehearsals with some fellow cast-members – most of them, as it happened, from the adjacent college of King's – he'd decided to share a beer with them in the bar of his own college, arrived at through the Junior Common Room. On entering he had been astonished to see a clapping, chanting circle of rowing hearties egging Tubs on as he negotiated the length of some polished magazine-strewn tables on a child's bicycle. Perhaps wisely, given his bulk, Tubs was not one of the students who negotiated his way round Cambridge on wheels. Now drunk, he was already wobbling perilously when he saw Simon at the door. He hailed him heartily with a wildly free arm, only to topple over, crushing the bike beneath himself and severely fracturing the piece of choice furniture which had been his 'track', while his crapulous cronies decided to do a bunk before what promised to be an almighty reckoning with the authorities. And indeed, as they (and, be it said, Simon's own actor pals from

King's) vanished into the night, a college porter, alerted by the uproar, had appeared at Simon's shoulder.

"Mr Heycock, sir?"

"Yes, Arthur?"

"What's going on?"

The answer was only too evident. Tubs lay moaning and groaning on the ground as he clutched his knee in a wreckage of wheels and mahogany.

"Er, just got here, Arthur. As I understand, some bastards from King's were trying to ride a bicycle across those tables. Mr Trumble here rather valiantly protested on behalf of the college and was set upon. I think we owe him our thanks, do we not?"

"You wouldn't know the names of those young gentlemen from King's, would you, sir?"

"'Fraid not, Arthur. Like I say – just got here myself."

Well, if the porter had his doubts, he let them be buried, and Tubs had survived to fight another day.

Here in Highgate, Simon wondered where this was all leading.

"The thing is, old chap, I've never been a great success with the ladies. D'you ever spot that?"

"Can't say as I did," said Simon with a commendably straight face. Frankly – notwithstanding memories of the redoubtable Daphne – he had sometimes wondered if Tubs was not still a virgin.

"But that Breeze!" continued Tubs. "What an absolute corker! Never knew an American girl before. Heavens – are they all so... *energetic*?"

"How would I know?"

"But, I mean, Hadley – "

Simon did not want to go there. "Tubs. What are you saying?"

"Was I? Oh right. Breeze! An absolute corker! I asked you here for a reason, old chap..." Again Tubs seemed suddenly bashful. "Thing is. I'm thinking of popping the question."

"Excuse me?"

"Tying the knot. Getting spliced. Making her my Life's Partner."

"Well, congratulations!"

"My question to you – why I asked you here – is will she say yea or nay. What do you think?"

"Perhaps you should ask her yourself."

"Do you think so, Simon?"

"If *you* think so, Tubs."

Tubs sipped hard on his drink, slowly put it down and then looked sentimentally at Simon. "Good old Simon. Always there with sound advice when I need him. Here's to you, old chap!" He raised his glass in a toast.

Simon reciprocated with a laugh. Had this really

been the big 'pow-wow'? To Simon – though evidently not to Tubs – it seemed a terrible anti-climax. He reached for one of Tubs's cigarettes but even as he did so sensed a thickening round his temples. He'd felt the threat of a headache since late afternoon and feared for the worst if he continued to keep pace with his friend's drinking. Without bothering to consult Tubs, who was now sprawled on the sofa in maudlin reflection, he wandered into the bathroom in search of a couple of aspirin. Reaching up for the medicine cabinet and twisting its lock, he was subjected to an avalanche of silver-foiled tablets. Sighing, he was joined in the doorway by Tubs.

"You all right, old man?"

"Good God, Tubs. Are you starting a collection?"

"You could say that." Tubs looked bashful for a second time.

"What in Heaven's name are they?"

"Anti-depressants."

Simon began to laugh, but suddenly checked himself. "You? – a depressive, Tubs? Tell me another one."

"Ah!" smiled Tubs. "Put not your faith in appearances, Simon my son. The clown who weeps? Not waving but drowning 'n' all that? You know the precedents. "

Simon had never realised his apparently happy-go-lucky friend had this side to him. Well, well, he pondered, deep old Tubs.

"But how come you've so many?"

"Truth be told, I came off them about the time, well, about the time I took up with Breeze. I just didn't stop my regular visits to the sawbones. Answered his daft questions with my regular nods and winks and kept on picking up the prescriptions."

"Whatever for?"

"Call it a hedge-fund? A little offshore investment?" Gently stacking the pills back in the medicine cabinet, Tubs turned the lock and steered Simon out of the bathroom. "I like to think it's all water under the bridge given present circumstances. But who knows?" he winked, a hand still on his friend's elbow. "We all have our rainy days."

The journey was pleasant, though Sarah had wanted to take her car and she was, in Simon's eyes, the worst driver in the world. How on earth, he wondered, had she ever passed her test? He could only imagine she had won over the examiner with her beauty and charm. Arriving amid a crashing of gears at an unpretentious but immensely comfortable hotel set quietly by itself in Hardy country, they had enjoyed luxurious baths in the en suite facilities, read novels for an hour or so (occasionally looking up to smile at each other) then taken dinner downstairs, where – amid stockbrokers and their wives – they had giggled softly at being so ostentatiously an Adulterous Couple. Afterwards they had gone straight to bed and it seemed on that first evening that their love-making, rudely interrupted so to speak by 'events', had now taken on a deeper, more meaningful rhythm, ceasing then taken up again in the night when both seemed to wake at the same time, renew tender recognition and reaffirm their fondness for each other.

For Simon this renewal was delicious but rather strange: he did not know that Sarah had reasons of her own – reasons parallel to his, as it happened – for not explaining the recent rupture in their relationship now magically healed, and in the absence of any more candid ventilation of the subject on either side he could only assume that there was some philosophy of life here, some attitude towards continuity and perseverance to which Sarah held the key and of which he, Simon, had yet to learn the existence.

At school he had always been a sprinter, finding those chums who were rugby forwards or long-distance runners to be poor fools pitiable in their failure to recognise not only the glamour but also the economy of effort enjoyed by wingers and 100-metre men like himself. Likewise, when he had experienced his one foray into dramaturgy – his well-received adaptation of the piece by Henry James – he'd come to realise that whilst classic stories often progress slowly, formally homologous with the protagonist's maturation, theatre plays tended to lurch abruptly from crisis to crisis – or at the very least from one event to the next. Not for him, he decided, that slow accumulation of layers, of 'patina' and texture.

He feared now that a similar impatience, sometimes confused with 'perfectionism', had come to characterise all his relationships. If he couldn't get it right quickly enough ('it' being what exactly in these relationships?), well, he'd move on – or was that back? – to another affair altogether or, failing that, to the consolations of his solitary life with its books, music and films. The notion of 'working at a partnership', of the 'long haul', was something he heard with a scepticism bordering on fear. Hadn't his own parents made just these compromises and been locked into a loveless marriage offering possibilities of loneliness no single man or woman could envisage?

So it was that in the face of such as Sarah – who, of course, had survived over twenty years of compromise with Zac – Simon wondered if he did not suffer a certain incapacity for life as understood by most others. Would his relationship with Hadley, he wondered, have blossomed into some long-term cohabitation or would this too have died prematurely on the vine?

On the morning after their arrival Sarah announced her determination to drive Simon out to a place she held particularly dear. A house with a watermill and a stream running by it.

"I grew up here," she said as they drew alongside. "I'd bring Zac here when we first knew each other."

"So you said."

"Do you mind?"

"Of course not." Simon squeezed her hand. "You want to stop? Look around?"

"Maybe tomorrow. This might seem crazy seeing as we've just got up but..."

"Yes?"

"Right now I'd like for us to go straight back to bed and fuck each other stupid."

"Who am I to disagree?"

Starting the car again with a bright nod, she pulled away, heading slowly up to the main road. But another car had turned off and was heading down towards them. A Bentley.

"Hey," said Simon as a joke. "That could almost be Zac."

And, unbelievably, Zac it was – his face taut behind the wheel with, next to him, a woman, her features too indistinct to read beneath the windscreen's glare.

Sarah must have spotted all this only a moment after Simon himself. Their car stalled and Zac's Bentley slid smoothly past and downhill without stopping or, it seemed, Zac casting so much as a sideways glance. Surely he had recognised Sarah's car? Surely he had identified her behind the wheel? Illogically, Sarah punched the horn and shouted "Zac!" over her shoulder – a cry that merely bounced back against the closed windows. What the hell was she hoping for? wondered Simon. Some cosy roadside *tête-à-tête* with polite introductions all round? But already the Bentley was out of sight.

Half an hour later, back in their hotel room, a now ferociously preoccupied Sarah punched numbers into her mobile as Simon stood bewildered by her side.

"Is this a good idea?" he began to ask lamely.

Clearly Zac – for there was no doubt it was him she was calling – had picked up on the other end. "What the fuck was that all about?" Sarah barked furiously into the phone. Simon was thinking the same – but as much of her call as of the encounter itself.

Sarah listened a moment. "Right. But remember in the future, *my* turf, *my* space." She signed off curtly.

"And the woman in the car?"

"Iris. So he says."

That night they did not make love. Sarah seemed possessed by some unarticulated churning rage and turned her back to him. In the morning she was her normal self, but made no mention of the incident. After a pleasant day exploring the countryside, its tea-rooms and antique shops, but keeping well clear of the millstream and its house, they drove back to London.

"So much for the idyllic short break", thought Simon and returned to his weekday life.

Hadley had not particularly enjoyed her abridged trip to Dorset with Zac. There had been a strange encounter – a moment when they had passed another car, almost scraping its side on a steep and narrow slip-road – after which Zac had received a short call on his mobile (were the events related? wondered Hadley. she couldn't see how) and then gone silent, fucking her efficiently that night before, still silent, turning away and falling instantly asleep. Next morning he explained the call on his mobile: some hiccough in the casting plans for his next production which meant he had to be back in London sooner than expected. He offered no details and Hadley spent the journey home privately measuring the passing countryside against childhood memories of a rolling Pennsylvania, its grim small towns alternating with glorious green hills. England, she decided, was still a children's playpen by comparison, heavily corralled and made up of cute little blocks – a paddock here, a stretch of arable land there – all locked into place and eventually circumscribed by an imminent coastline just out of sight. In her childhood, Butler at least, where her family vacationed away from the bustle of Pittsburgh, was only a Main Street's distance from ecstatic horse-rides to a limitless horizon, the wind whipping her face and, yes, somewhere back beyond her shoulder, her parents, also on horseback, reining in with a combination of pride and fear, letting her and her horse Brewster have their head. "Hell," they seemed to say, "we can't nanny her forever." Pleasantly enough, no accidents had occurred, no ghastly falls, no spine-shattering upsets. Brewster was almost older than herself with a wisdom all his own, as if the horse were looking out for the rider and not the rider the horse.

How different, then, from these sleek dark English fields tapering off to deserted, garishly-lit High Streets through commuter dormitory-towns, Little Chef diners and motorway complexes which seemed to be imitating paintings by Edward Hopper but couldn't even get that right.

No champion of America *per se*, having inherited from her parents a liberal contempt for much of its foreign policy, Hadley nonetheless knew the temptation of seeing the UK as an inevitable second best to the US, knew she too on occasion had slipped into what sympathetic but sometimes beady Brit friends considered America's sense of 'entitlement' – forever first in line, forever the gold standard by which other nations were to be judged. But, shoot, wasn't her awareness of this the seed of her coming to live in the UK in the first place?

Brits might have bad teeth (so her sisters back in America were always jokingly reminding her), they might seem almost maddeningly old-fashioned in their technological oh-bugger-me-we'll-just-muddle-through primitivism, their daughters might grow up so sexually ill-educated that teenage pregnancies checked in at an astonishing rate, and yet, and yet, she had sensed and found here a benevolence, a fortitude and – yes – there was no other word for it, a *sweetness* she had come to treasure.

As for her own chosen field of endeavour, acting, well, the Brits had it licked. Perhaps their drama conservatoires could not deliver with the same high voltage as the Yanks when it came to Naturalism. Perhaps Brits seemed underpowered when it came to musicals. But, boy, when it came to other aspects of the repertoire – the stylisations of Restoration Comedy, the demands of the Shakespearian iambic – they seemed to have written the book. As indeed, from a certain point of view, they had. Wasn't Zac himself – relatively unknown in the US – a shining example of what British practice could aspire to?

Thus Hadley ruminated as Zac concluded their journey, now negotiating the outskirts of London and – she suddenly realised – taking her through the grubby streets of the suburb she had made her home these last two years. He pulled up just as her remembrance of that fondness for all things English, for Zac himself, led her to squeeze his left arm with affection. He did not respond.

"I'll drop you off here then," he said, not cutting the engine.

"You won't come in? Have a drink or...?" But already she sensed the answer.

"No. Busy day ahead. This casting problem for one thing." He pecked her on the cheek, now at last granting her a brief smile. "Catch up with you tomorrow?"

And already she was out of the car, locating the dark house where she was a lodger, a transient, a stranger in a strange land.

"Sure thing." She nodded and, closing the door, walked off briskly with her shoulder bag banging her hip.

When she reached the front door she looked back. Zac's Bentley had already glided on, its flared tail lights diminishing rapidly.

Sarah slid quietly into a seat in a corner of the rehearsal room, a draughty church hall in Belsize Park. It seemed that practically the whole cast, some eight or nine, was there, though all but two of them were not called for this particular scene. The writer — in this case Iris — was just gathering up bag, script and mobile phone and leaving for another appointment. Passing Sarah on the way out, she smiled graciously, trailed a quick "How lovely to see you" and was gone. Was Iris's departure pure coincidence, wondered Sarah, or had Zac mentioned she'd be 'dropping by'? Ostensibly, ex-wife and new partner enjoyed an 'adult understanding', but much had gone unsaid and unforgiven between them. What, if anything, Iris had made of the incident in Dorset she couldn't begin to imagine.

Sarah looked back on that day with a confused flush of shame. She had overreacted to Zac's being there. She had taken it out on Simon. And she had belatedly come to accept that she had done so because she had ended up comparing these two lovers, past and present, and found the present one — manifestly the better person — wanting. And now here she was again in the eyes of the world paying homage at the altar of Zac's creativity!

Script in hand, Zac was standing in a large chalk-marked rectangle between a young actor and actress.

Light on his feet, weaving slightly between the two of them, he was once again the college scrum-half.

"John," he asked. "Who's running this scene? You or Susie here?"

"Umm... me?"

Zac turned to the actress. "Susie. What do *you* think?"

"Oh, I rather thought it was me," she answered. Her subsequent laughter was shared moderately by Zac, John and the onlookers.

"Okay," continued Zac, now standing by Susie a moment. "What are you doing with the line 'You have nice teeth, Bill'?"

"I'm flattering? I'm charming?" asked Susie.

"And the next line? Read the next line."

Susie did so. "'Are they your own?'" A ripple of amusement passed through the onlookers who, however, had already heard this line several times by now.

"So *now* what are you doing, Susie?"

"I'm putting him down? I'm discouraging him?"

Zac moved closer to the other actor. "What does 'Bill' think?"

"Bill thinks he's being challenged?" asked John.

"And?" prompted Zac.

"And then again he thinks – perhaps – he's being flirted with?"

Zac nodded and smiled. "I think Bill might be right." He turned to the actress. "Susie? Not a put-down? Rather a provocation? You're challenging *and* you're flirting?"

Susie nodded. Zac stood back a couple of paces and the actors took the lines again. This time when they'd finished they didn't need to be told they'd got it right – they knew already. Zac stepped back further without comment, merely nodding for them to continue. At last, for a brief second, he relaxed his focus and, seeing Sarah the other side of the room, held up a hand in greeting.

Same old Zac, thought Sarah. Did she originally fall in love with him for just this ability, an ability on show even at a routine rehearsal such as this? At that time she'd have praised it as 'charisma', as yet not aware as she later became that charisma (which could occasionally be brutal) was not the same as 'charm' (which could occasionally be vapid) and the two were mutually exclusive despite her need for now one, now the other in her life. Wasn't this all the difference between Zac and Simon? Not quite, she would grudgingly admit: her early years with Saul had led her to enjoy being present if not at the epicentre of artistic power at least in its first circle and Zac was, in his world, no less at the centre of things than Saul. But Simon, by comparison? This charming but uncharismatic intellectual whose cleverness commanded respect only among fellow-academics – where did that leave *him*? Sarah blushed to think how she had first introduced him to her son as an 'award-winning writer', which was not untrue as it happened (that ghost-story he'd adapted had picked up the odd accolade), but why, so nakedly, did she feel the need to have a player, a celebrity, a star on her arm? Was it ultimately an index of her own feeling of worthlessness?

Zac brought the rehearsal to its close. He and Sarah retired to a nearby greasy-spoon café, still just open. This meeting between them had been postponed, then postponed again since... when? wondered Sarah. Before Christmas at least. It was about Sophie – or, more precisely, Sophie's college fees – and hence had to be arranged in her absence as indeed in that of Iris, who, as Sarah saw it, would be at best irrelevant and at worst an obstacle, since she'd be batting for Zac.

It seemed they'd silently agreed to draw a veil over the Dorset incident.

"So how have you been?" asked Zac, leaning back against the partition and beginning to stroke the ring on his little finger.

"Very well. Excellent." So simple a question, thought Sarah, but always so difficult to negotiate. If she oversold her present self-sufficiency Zac would need greater persuading when it came to parting with money for Sophie's expenses; if she came on too negative about her new 'solo' life it would flatter him, suggesting that things had turned sour the moment Zac had removed his beneficent presence. "Excellent, that is, except for certain financial pressures."

"In particular?" Zac took a sip at his his café latte.

"Oh come on, darling!" Even now, after so many years of antagonism and a divorce in all but name, she still found herself slipping into terms of endearment which had become second nature to her. "Sophie's got college fees to pay. Accommodation to find."

"So how much are we looking at?"

Sarah quoted a figure and Zac raised his eyebrows.

"I'm not asking for all of it, of course."

"Well thank you."

She chose to ignore the sarcastic tone. "Sophie is your daughter too. I think I've the right to ask for a goodly contribution." Zac had gone quiet, contemplating his coffee-cup. "Zac?"

Finally he nodded. "Fair enough. I *had* been thinking about a new car."

"What's wrong with the Bentley?"

"I had been thinking Iris and I should buy somewhere bigger."

Sarah waited a moment. "And?"

"So be it," Zac finally conceded. "Fifty-fifty?"

She didn't quite know what to say. It was at least an offer, but then, apart from the income on a property – now rented out – which she'd managed to buy in the days of Saul she had no income as such, while Zac was on – what? Fifty thousand a year?

"Would you consider upping that a little?" she finally asked.

"How so?"

"Listen – I don't have a salary like you."

"Nor do you have a new mortgage like mine. Besides, you could always do something about that lack of salary."

"What do you mean?" Sarah recognised a certain feral set to Zac's jaw familiar from scenes of previous confrontation.

"Well, after all – what do you do all day? Very little as far as I can see. Why not get yourself a job like the rest of humanity? Hey, I know – why not start a B & B right there in the house?"

"Are you serious?"

"Fucking right I am."

Sarah felt an urge to throw her cappuccino in his face. She was all the more piqued in that there was a grain of truth in what he'd said: she did do 'very little' all day, at least since she'd stopped producing the odd fringe-show and playing small parts in BBC dramatisations. But then how, at the age she was now, could she seriously undertake new 'career options'?

"And you, Zac? When are *you* going to join the rest of humanity? When are you going to hand in your membership card to the Society of Perpetual Adolescents? I thought when we adopted Sophie you'd at last grow up, accept some sense of responsibility. Clearly I was wrong."

They stared hotly at each other for a moment, then both looked away.

"Okay," said Zac finally. "Sixty-forty. The best I can do."

Sarah nodded in a gesture of finality, "Fine. Thank you." But now she saw that Zac had started to smile.

"Hey" he said, "I'd forgotten how beautiful you are when you're angry. Want me to drive you home?"

9

Simon had led his students through the final phase of his course, those years which had stretched from Conrad's apocalyptic *Heart of Darkness* at the century's end to *The Secret Agent* of 1907, years of unprecedented internationalism culminating in deracinated militants threatening the privileged Western order. Now, exactly one hundred years later, were we better equipped, he asked, to see, well, if not a shape at least piquant modern-day parallels?

As ever, this last sprint to a conclusion had seemed to Simon both rushed and glib, but then at this point the academic year as a whole always seemed to move ridiculously fast. Images of lemmings and Gadarene swine came to mind. And then what? wondered Simon. Another year? Another year beyond that? Some new kind of apocalypse or just more of the same? Macro to micro. The weighty to the trivial... The trip to Dorset with Sarah had left a bitter aftertaste. How could it be, wondered Simon, that such a bizarre coincidence – for it was as such that he read the encounter with Zac's car in Devon – how could it be that such a peripheral, freakish, ultimately negligible event should somehow poison the well of goodwill and affection that he had rediscovered with Sarah after their earlier separation from each other?

He had rung her up a day after their return and politely but succinctly she had deferred any subsequent meeting pleading a busy schedule. *What* schedule? wondered Simon. God knows, it wasn't his fault if her ex-husband chose to go visiting one of their old love-haunts on the very same day! But Simon somehow intuited that from this moment he and Sarah would never again sleep together.

Whenever he found himself depressed his first instinct was to retreat into sleep and, thereafter, to immerse himself in the things he had first loved as a young adult. For the most part this meant jazz, films and French literature. Why had he not studied this last at university? he sometimes asked himself. At least it might have been a passport to another life, lived, he liked to fantasise, among the cobbled gradients of the Left Bank or the deep mauve-greens of Provence.

Now he pulled down a battered copy of one particular novel that had always been dear to him.

He travelled.

He came to know the melancholy of the steamboat, the cold awakening in the tent, the tedium of landscapes and ruins, the bitterness of interrupted friendship.

He returned.

He went into society, and he had other loves.

Simon snapped the book shut and did a quick calculation. The savings he'd invested plus what he'd get for his flat plus his pension plus some sort of early retirement package... Why not? he thought. Why ever not?

But it was typical of life – or at least *his* life, he thought – that like some cocker spaniel who's feeling neglected or undervalued it should take a snap at his ankles just as he was turning away.

Three weeks before the end of term, Simon set his students their last assignment. A week later, when class was ended and all the other students scattered, it was the 'front-row' American who came up to him.

"Professor Heycock?"

"Hi, Annette. How can I help?"

"It's about the assignment you set?"

"What's the problem?"

"You've asked us to consider how far Modernism would be 'both a step forward and a step back'?"

"Correct."

"I'm having, like, difficulties with this. Hey – this is so, like, *imposing* of me – but I wondered if I could buy you a coffee next door?"

Simon checked his watch. "Well – I am on a fairly tight schedule," he lied. "Er – just ten minutes?"

They sat in a partitioned booth in the local sandwich bar. Simon had given her more than ten minutes: how literature had bifurcated a century before into 'middlebrow' and 'highbrow', how the robust tradition of the socially inclusive novel had remained with the like of Galsworthy, Wells and Bennett whilst experimentation, inwardness and, arguably, elitism would be the path of Joyce, Woolf and Faulkner (authors, as it happened, Simon was especially fond of), thereby looping back in some ways to an earlier pre-Austen epoch, to the private and isolated voices of *Pamela, Clarissa* et al.

Annette, who had been scribbling furiously throughout while maintaining a fixed smile, now looked up.

"Well, I guess that's my understanding of the question," concluded Simon. "Perhaps I've said too much. You were meant to have figured this out for yourself."

"Wow," said Annette, capping her felt-tip. "Awesome."

"Then again nothing more than I've already said in class."

Flicking back through her notes, Annette nodded a final time and looked him in the eyes. "Profess... Simon. Mind if I get, like, real *personal*?"

Simon already feared what was coming. "Yes, Annette?"

"I don't know how to put this. I've got, like, a kinda *crush* on you?"

"Ah."

" Would this be – Jesus, now I'm embarrassed – would this be *reciprocated*?"

Simon tried to smile brightly. Where should he begin? "I'm really flattered, Annette. You're a beautiful, intelligent young woman..."

"But?"

"But I'm, er, otherwise involved."

"You married, Simon?"

"No, but..."

"But you've got, like, a Significant Other?"

"You could say that."

Annette smiled ruefully. "Hey – you can't blame a girl for trying?" With a slight sigh she put away her pen and pad. "Maybe you're right. After all, you said it yourself..."

"Excuse me?"

"Maybe a step forward is also a step back?"

Simon laughed and, paying for the coffees, felt only a twinge of regret – but a twinge all the same. Had he underrated this buoyant, uncomplicated young woman? And wasn't it just typical that when he was still reeling from the encounter with Hadley a second bus, so to speak, should come along so soon, unsolicited and unwished for? Anyway who was he kidding – 'Otherwise involved'? 'A Significant Other'?

He watched Annette's retreating back as she disappeared down the road. Did he wish to change his mind? "Too late, Simon," he told himself. "Too late."

Zac's new production was met with mixed reviews: broadly speaking, praise for the direction and acting, condemnation for the play itself. Iris went into a three-day spin of depression and anger which Zac coped with as best he knew how. In this case it amounted to his taking advantage of Iris's sulky absence from certain performances to arrange for Hadley to see the show. Or was it, Hadley wondered, to arrange for the show to see *her*? That the actors and theatre-personnel knew where this pretty American figured in the scheme of things was surely not in doubt and Zac made no attempt to pretend otherwise. Had she not become his 'trophy girlfriend', earning him brownie-points for proving to be once again (what was the Brit phrase?) 'a bit of a lad'?

If truth be told, such unvoiced questions were starting to crowd in quite frequently now, but curiously the beginnings of disaffection with Zac had started with Hadley herself – a feeling of mild self-loathing which became increasingly pronounced as she stretched out on sofa or bed of an afternoon and watched trash TV while Zac pottered around, sometimes clothed, sometimes not, occasionally peeking over her shoulder at another re-run of *Friends* or some programme on house-renovation before making an ironic comment ("Ah, the intellectual relaxes!") and moving on back to his rehearsal notes or phone calls.

Wasn't this what she'd done as a sulky teenager? A kind of pointless absorption in nothing whatever which had blocked out her father, consigning him to the status of redundant, purposeless bystander, as if to say "Hey – you offering anything better?" Why was she doing this now with her lover? On such afternoons – afternoons which at the beginning of their relationship had been gleeful and illicit because it was time snatched away from Iris – their occupation of the same living-space seemed less like amicable cohabitation, a chummy absence of the need to say or do anything together, than a mute recognition that, well, there was nothing more to say or do together when they were no longer fucking or eating or consorting with some theatrical third party of Zac's acquaintance.

The memory of Franzee and her nemesis – her appointment with Dark Destiny – had at the time allowed Hadley some obscure rationale for her decision to meet up again with Zac while aware of the probable consequences. But it did not give her reasons for so abruptly throwing over Simon. In the short time she'd known him hadn't he been generous and attentive to a fault – loving even, in his laconic way? As time moved on, Hadley's failure to find any justification for behaviour she would have condemned in others proved irksome to her. And increasingly, as she settled into the routine of a once-a-week assignation with Zac (hands open wide, he would explain this was the best he could do given commitments to work and to Iris), she wondered what else could have driven her to such an uncharacteristic act. She had dumped boyfriends back in the US just as she herself had been dumped, but like sex on the back seat of automobiles – God help her, even on occasion in movie-houses – it was all part of growing up as a teenager in America, something she'd blush to remember though easily shrug off. But this was different and with time on her hands (Breeze for one seemed much taken up with Tubs these days) she had the opportunity to ponder the whole business and arrive at the conclusion that it all came down to Danger and Glamour, each seductive of itself but, like brandy and champagne, lethal when combined.

Danger not simply because there was something flagrantly transgressive of all proprieties, all 'correctness', all civilised good taste in Zac's sexuality. No, more than this, the suggestion to anyone taking him on that this well-known cock-artist would respect no one and nobody in his urge to get laid. Zac was scarcely Byron, but social primitivism had proved its appeal in both cases.

As for the Glamour, this was the part that worried Hadley most. Reluctantly she had come to accept that it was finally Zac's celebrity, his well-earned reputation in the theatre that made all the difference. Did she wish to boast about the liaison? Not particularly. Did she as an actress wish to get work from him? Only if he too should wish it. But still there was the novelty, the thrill, of her – an outsider to the UK – colliding like some rogue meteor with this substantial planet in the British theatrical galaxy. The downside, she wryly concluded, was twofold. First, there was a lot of other debris – Iris and Zac's ex-wife to name just two

– floating out there in his gravitational pull. Secondly, the closer you got to it, the more all glamour faded. When the most powerful, the most beautiful expected you, literally or metaphorically, to wash their socks, it was only a matter of time before the glamour became a memory only refreshed in the star-struck admiration of those who, enjoying no such proximity, knew no better.

These days such reflections invariably brought her back to Simon. What was he doing now? Who was he with?

"I thought I might go see Breeze," she said instead one particular afternoon.

"Mm. When would that be?"

"Later today. This evening perhaps."

"I thought we were having a drink with Dan and Leonie."

"Ah. Right."

"Of course, if you'd prefer to see your friends rather than mine..."

"Is that so bad?"

"Not at all. Your choice."

And off he wandered again, flicking open his mobile to check that all was well at the office. Such a call was surely for her benefit, she surmised, the Action reading 'I hereby suggest indifference – because I have another life, a profession... unlike some I could mention!'

"Do I bore you, Zac?" she asked when he was done.

"Bore me? No. You're Low Maintenance. I like it."

"What's *High* Maintenance?"

"Needing to be entertained. Needing to be diverted."

"Cool. Then perhaps I'll be off right away."

"So be it. Then we'll speak tomorrow? Oh did I tell you?" he added casually. "Next week I'm going to Sarajevo."

"No, you didn't tell me."

"*War Casualties*. We've arranged a few interviews."

Zac was preparing, Hadley knew, a piece of 'verbatim' theatre where those who'd suffered in conflicts, civilians and military alike, recalled their traumas on tape. Edited and re-structured, they'd be read later by a group of actors.

"How long will you be away?"

Zac shrugged. "A week, give or take."

"You won't forget about Mom and Elliot on Friday, will you?"

"Of course not."

Tubs still hadn't managed to 'pop the question'. Somehow, what with his shyness, Breeze's garrulous enthusiasm and, well, their funny good times together, the moment never seemed right. And he was aware that her year in the UK was coming to an end. God forbid she should go back to LA! For Tubs, who had been to the US only briefly and then solely to New York, LA sounded impossibly alien, as unreal as, say, Japan. To be condemned to go back there seemed the kind of fate from which any young lady, let alone 'his' Breeze, needed rescuing. True, he hadn't, conversely, exposed her to West Sussex and the Aged Parents (what *would* they make of her? he chortled) but he'd cross that bridge when they came to it.

Meanwhile how robust Breeze continued to be! How uncluttered and uncomplex in her attitude to life in general and him in particular! And if this entailed a certain benign bossiness as of Tubs being taken in charge by a sexy matron – one who turned up at his office when she chose and, to the raised eyebrows of Tubs's colleagues, whisked him off loudly for cocktails here or a jazz-concert there; one who allowed herself to tease him for his 'sad-ass' Brit stuffiness, his Dickensian turns of phrase ("Crikey!" "Blimey!" were high on the list) or censoriously prod his 'gross' belly – well, he loved her the more for it.

And there was something else. Beneath her bravado he found that Breeze was far less at ease with sex than could be assumed. If for others this might pose a problem – it was not that she didn't like it or hesitate to engage in it, simply there was a self-consciousness here, an unexpected anxiety as of someone always on the point of asking "Am I doing this right?" – for Tubs it was a relief to know his own relative lack of experience was appreciated and mirrored. He'd never be a stud, but now this was wonderfully irrelevant: both partners could relax and be tenderly complicit in the knowledge that a trusting heart and a willingness to please were more important than expertise.

Heavens above! Such was his new lease of life, he thought, he might even give up smoking.

Later that same week Zac sat at his desk in a very different mood from that of Tubs. He was pondering. Did he really want to meet Hadley's parents? The invitation was for two hours hence. What would he tell these respectable mid-Americans? That he relished fucking their daughter up the arse? That he felt 'great affection' for her – despite having an undivorced wife, a mistress he was now living with, and a series of girlfriends which had not stopped when he moved in with present mistress and of which their daughter was certainly not the last? My oh my, he thought grimly. This was shaping up to be a great evening.

Meanwhile, a deeply apprehensive Hadley sat in The Ivy opposite her mother and stepfather. What a ridiculously fashionable restaurant this was! Wasn't that – over at a distant table – the National Theatre's present King Lear? Well, he certainly seemed to be tucking into his main course with a royal appetite. Her parents were here on a European trip taking in Paris, Rome and before that, London. It was they who had sweetly suggested this supper-party.

"He *is* a little old, darling," said her mother.

"Hey," replied Hadley with some spirit. "What's the age gap between you and Elliot?"

Elliot had the good grace to laugh, her mother too – not without adding, "Honey, Elliot and I are the same generation at least."

"Jesus, Mom. You always taught me to be open, to be loving. So as it happens, the man I'm open to, the man I... care for, he's older than me. So what? Can I only date certain people? What about people who are crippled? People who are sick? I should give them a wide berth?"

Momentarily – and a shade comically, thought Hadley – her mother looked stricken. "Heavens. Zac isn't sick, is he? Zac isn't..."

"Of course not!"

Squeezing his wife's forearm, Elliot chose the moment to intervene. "Honey. All Hadley is saying is..."

"I know what Hadley's saying," sighed her mother. "I just think... well..."

"Yes?" asked Hadley.

"It's only because" — it was her mother's turn to squeeze some flesh — "we love you and want the best for you."

"I know that. Thank you." Hadley was moved despite herself.

Suddenly her mobile rang. It was Zac. She listened, said "Okay" and shut it down again. Her parents looked at her expectantly. Could they begin to fathom how humiliated she felt?

"That was Zac. He sends his apologies but he can't make it. Something about preparations for his trip? People still to see?"

To their credit, her mother and stepfather exchanged no looks, merely studying the linen tablecloth. After a pause it was Elliot who nodded and reached for the menu. "Too bad. Hadley? What did you fancy for *hors d'oeuvre*?"

"Ah yes. The National Library. It was shelled by the Serbs, you know? An act of gratuitous, spiteful vandalism."

Zac sat listening to the half-dozen individuals ranged on chairs around him. Spring was on its way, but it was cold in this backroom of the State Theatre and he pulled his coat more tightly in on himself before continuing to make notes in his small black pad. The woman speaking, name of Katja, was in her late thirties with honey-coloured hair and dark eyes.

"The National Library," she continued, "had stood on the banks of the river for a hundred years or more. What was inside was much, much older, going back centuries. It contained all our treasures. That library was Sarajevo's memory. That library was our culture and our soul." She paused a moment, as if remembering fondly.

Zac prompted her gently. "You were there when it was bombed?"

The woman shook her head. "No, thank God. But I was here in the city, I'd just left the conservatoire. What people remember most was the smell of paper burning and, for days after, the ashes from the books, drifting through the air like thick black snow."

"I was here too that day," piped up another, quite sparkily. "I'd been rehearsing Hamlet!"

"He would have been a great *great* Hamlet!" whispered a third to general assent.

Zac felt a sudden urge to weep. The man who was to play Hamlet and seemed quite jolly was sitting in a wheelchair. He had no legs.

At the end of the long day's work and as evening fell, Zac took the actor – his name was Stefan – for a walk, solemnly pushing the heavy wheelchair through the market-place where darkness was held at bay by a row of tiny glass-fronted interiors, havens of reassurance in which hanging oil-lamps spilled ribs of light across crimson Turkish carpets, copper plates, even – so long after the 'events'– some remaining burnished shell-cases etched with a delicate Moorish filigree.

Stefan seemed more tired than he had been earlier in the day. Was this, wondered Zac, the result of his condition? God, to be stuck in a wheelchair hour after hour, day after day, always below the eye-level of anyone standing, always straining to look upward! But somehow, despite this tiredness, the mere fact of not facing his interlocutor – Zac behind him like a hovering but 'invisible' psychoanalyst – seemed to free Stefan up. He began, cryptically enough, with a quotation.

"What is a man
If his chief good and market of his time
Be but to sleep and feed?"

Zac completed the passage. *"A beast, no more?"*

"Perhaps." Stefan chuckled mirthlessly. "You believe this?"

Zac's shrug went unobserved. He continued to negotiate the crowd, passers-by who had been looking elsewhere suddenly looming up and nearly stumbling across the wheelchair and its occupant's lap, others side-stepping at the last moment with tight, embarrassed smiles.

"So tell me again what is the work you are preparing, Zac?"

"It's a show on those who have survived war, conflict, trauma."

"A show?"

"The wrong word perhaps. An evening where we give voice to those who have suffered."

"And such people – they do not have a voice already?"

"They do. They do indeed. But it's not perhaps a voice heard too often in the places I come from."

"You mean the places where you entertain?"

"If 'entertain' is the word."

"Ah. Then what is your word? Why *are* you there? To inform? To instruct? To teach?"

Zac was not sure if he knew the answer to this and let it pass.

"You know something, my friend? You are the best of the English. You are not like your politicians, your stockbrokers or your money-makers." Before Zac had time to demur, Stefan went on. "But the tragedy of you English – and I mean, like you, the best of you English – is that you know no tragedy."

"How so?"

"You do not weep. You just do not feel happy. You do not rejoice. You just feel less unhappy than you felt before. You do not even kill. You simply refuse to give life."

Zac felt wounded. He had no children of his own. His low sperm-count had seen to that.

"And so you turn," continued Stefan. "You look around. You say who has suffered, who has wept, rejoiced, even killed? And when you find who has – in Central or South America, in Africa, in Eastern and Middle Europe and now perhaps in Afghanistan, Iraq – of this suffering too, even of this you are envious, this too you would seek to make your own. Why not? You have colonised everything else."

Now the cathedral bells were tolling in a pleasing discord with the wail of the muezzin, visible on a minaret less than fifty metres distant. Zac pushed the wheelchair on, stung and aggrieved by Stefan's words. "Are you telling me my work, this project, it's just so much pissing in the wind?"

"No. Not at all. I repeat – you and your kind are the best of Western Europe. Only I will ask of you what I ask of myself – what I should have asked before, in a sense, my life" – he gestured to his missing legs – "it came to an end. This your time here on earth, was this the best you could make of it? The most meaningful? The most worthy? You know, here in our country the gypsies have a saying. They say: 'The winter will ask what you did in the summer.'" He paused a moment, almost laughed. "Well, my friend? What will you say? What did you do in the summer of your life?"

That evening Zac sat drinking with two or three of the other actors in one of those atmospheric cafés which it seemed to him Central Europe did so well. Stefan had cried off, pleading a need to rest, but Zac could not get him out of his mind. Surely by any standards the actor had been grossly unfair; at least in his own way and as best he could, Zac was responding to the sort of criticism implied there. How many others could say as much? How many others were putting on work about *Bosnia*, for fuck's sake?

But his discontents would not entirely disappear. "Jesus," thought Zac, finally surrendering to the weight of Stefan's rhetoric. "We spend our lives worrying about the next production, the next grant-cut, the next fuck, and in a place like this people live on through carnage and chaos, the arbitrary victims of History, of – what was the phrase? – its 'spiteful vandalism'."

Nevertheless, his sobering reflections did not prevent him, later that evening, from propositioning Katja and taking her to bed.

"You fucked a *war casualty*?"

"She was not a 'war casualty'! She was just one of the witnesses we interviewed." Zac was exasperated. Wasn't it always agreed they'd be open about who they slept with? First he gets attacked by that actor in Sarajevo, and now...

Hadley nodded as if yielding a point. But then in his absence she'd already come to a decision. This man who had promised he'd leave his present partner for her. This man who seemed to have some moral gene missing. What had she been imagining in all their weeks together? That he'd 'settle down'? That he'd 'turn over a new leaf'? She looked away and whispered something under her breath.

"Say that again." Suddenly he had grasped her wrist with the same alarming tightness she'd known when she had produced the vibrator.

"Listen..."

"Say that again."

"I said, I think it's over."

"And?"

"And what?"

Zac was furious. "Are you telling me there's no one else?"

"You gonna beat up on me, Zac? Resort to violence? Hey, didn't you once do a show on a housing estate, battered wives, Neanderthal husbands 'n' all? "

"So there *is* no one else?"

"No," she said and Zac slightly eased his hold. "There is no one else." But now Hadley felt a surge of screw-you defiance. "Except, yes, there was."

"Ah." He let go of her entirely now and seemed to ponder a moment, manically stroking the ring on his little finger. "Now we have it. You're going back to him? To her? To whoever they are?"

"I don't know. Let's say I made a mistake."

"The time spent with me? That was a mistake?"

"No. Leaving him. And, yes, it is a 'him'."

Zac stepped a pace or so away. He glared a moment, unseeingly, at the window. "So tell me the worst. Someone you knew. Someone I know? Another director?"

"Listen. Can't we just -"

"I said, 'Another director'?"

"No."

"An actor?"

"No."

"A writer then?" God help us! thought Zac. A sudden vision of that smooth bastard Robert Donniger – *Sir* Robert Donniger, no less! – passed before his eyes.

"No." Oh for Christ's sake, why not just tell him and be done with it? "Simon Heycock."

"What?"

"Simon Heycock. He's a..."

"I know who he bloody is!" Zac sat down again abruptly. "I think he's been fucking my wife for years."

Hadley was more shocked than she cared to show. "Hey, you mean Iris?"

"No. Sarah."

Suddenly she felt an irresistible urge to laugh.

"What's so funny?"

"I had no idea. Really."

"Well now you do. May it bring you great joy."

Hadley shook her head as of someone defeated by colossal circumstance. Simon? Sweet Simon? She scrolled back. That first phone call he'd taken in the Baker Street pub? That was from her? That sense she'd sometimes got of another in his recent past, another of whom he never spoke? That was her too?

In his office later that day Zac was, in the eyes of his co-workers, more than usually unbearable. He sat at his desk, the door closed, seeing no one and answering no calls. When Tina looked in to see if he wanted a coffee, he positively barked at her to leave him alone. Not for the first time, she thought seriously about 'reconsidering her position'.

Only towards the end of the afternoon did some semblance of civility return. Zac, looking a little sheepish now about his earlier tantrum, walked through and asked sweetly if the last post had already gone.

Two days later Simon received through the mail a plain brown envelope, addressed in a tight, rather cramped hand. He didn't recognise the writing, nor was there any note inside. Instead was the sort of photograph – ill-framed, badly lit – that had been taken with a delayed shutter, the subjects composing themselves quickly back in front of the camera. It was of a laughing Hadley, stretched naked across the lap of Zac, himself clothed.

Simon was astonished, and spent the rest of the morning sorting out his emotions. Why had Hadley never told him about an affair with Zac? Ruefully, he accepted it was for the same reasons he had never told Hadley about Sarah. But who was the anonymous 'well-wisher' who had sent the photo? Simon was perplexed, but also upset. He had begun, with some pain, to write Hadley out of his life and this new occurrence picked like a dirty fingernail at a wound which was starting to heal.

And then he had another thought – slow in coming, he had to admit. Did Zac know for certain about the relationship with Sarah? The two of them had never been caught *in flagrante* but the guy was no fool. In such a case might it not be Zac himself who'd sent this? For the first time that day, Simon almost smiled. This was getting like some crazy farce – or, at the very least, a re-working of *La Ronde*. Whatever next?

This is the 'next' that Simon foresaw. (In another context he'd have called it 'proleptic'.)

He would be in a crowded theatre foyer – a first night, say. Zac and he would brush shoulders, both turn and instantly start shouting at each other. They would only stop when dragged away by their respective partners. Half the theatre community of London would have been witness to this and it would fuel gossip for, well, at least a day.

Or...

One of them would be seated, deep in conversation, at a restaurant table (preferably on the pavement outside?) The other would begin to walk past, look down and stare. Whoever was standing would pick up the drink of the seated one. And throw it over his face. (But who would be the seated and who the standing?)

Or...

Passing each other in the street, Zac and he would nod curtly at each other. One or other would then feel a tap on his shoulder and, turning, receive a punch full on the mouth. (Again, who the aggressor and who the victim?)

Or any combination of these?

In the event, the Big Showdown would be the Big

Nothing-Very-Much. And, indeed, there would be a sizeable delay.

Some weeks later Zac's show, rechristened *Witnesses*, surfaced at a Fringe theatre. It was a three-performance affair, hastily assembled in the 'verbatim' tradition with just a bunch of actors sitting on a bare stage, reading from their transcripts. But, regardless of its provenance, Simon had wanted to see it and Sarah, he gathered, had already seen it at the first night. He went alone.

In the interval he was standing outside the theatre. It was a mild evening, already with promise of summer, and he was eating an ice-cream when Zac walked past in the direction of the stage door with two vaguely recognisable actors and the partner ('Iris'?) Simon had seen at Mark's wrap party.

Zac passed, then looked back, momentarily allowing his companions to walk on.

"Zac?"

"Simon?"

"What can I say? Good work." However inappropriate to the moment, Simon was conceding no more than the truth.

Zac paused. "Thanks. Right. Thanks..."

But already Iris was coming back with a bemused expression. She took him by the arm and, nodding politely, was leading him away before Simon could find further words.

"Who was that?" whispered Iris, squeezing his elbow.

"No one," said Zac, still within earshot. "Just some academic."

And there perhaps things might have rested. But just as the outrageous photo had quickened Simon's emotions in regard to Hadley, so this more anodyne encounter seemed to spark Zac into a delayed frenzy. That smug Simon Heycock, with his fucking ice-cream! Well, he'd see about that. For a start, Sarah could go whistle for her 'sixty-forty'. As for Hadley, well...

10

Mark stood opposite the sofa on which his mother, a little tearful, was seated. He was furious.

"What does he mean he's broke?"

"The new flat? The flat with Iris? This and other expenses, well, they've left him a bit short, he says."

"How short? How much does he owe you?"

"A couple of grand."

"*A couple of grand?*"

"Well, three more like. It wouldn't matter except..."

"What do you mean, 'it wouldn't matter'?"

"Except there are Sophie's college fees coming up. Accommodation fees as well."

"Sophie is his daughter as well as yours."

"I know, but... " Sarah trailed off, looking away. Why, she wondered, was she put in the position of having to defend Zac? Why was she, it seemed, bearing the brunt of Mark's anger?

"Bloody typical!" he barked, only to be hushed by a gesture from Sarah – elsewhere in the house the weekly cleaner was at work. He turned away, feeling tears of rage welling up inside him. "How much did you say?"

"Listen. I shouldn't have mentioned it."

"Why ever not? It's outrageous."

Mark suppressed the feeling he had sometimes acknowledged that no man would be good enough for his mother, let alone the Worm. He hurried on to another, more comforting thought: he'd always hated Zac and, if not before, here was validation of that hatred. He pulled out a cheque book.

"Listen. Mark. Please."

"We are talking about my sister after all. Please take this. As for Zac himself..." He snorted dismissively and rattled off his signature. "Here. I can afford it."

Sarah nodded gratefully. He had made out a sum well above what she had quoted. As she folded it away she wryly concluded that the worst of this was not the money issue itself. It was that she could never talk calmly to her closest flesh-and-blood about the man she had once loved.

Hadley had had it with Zac and, for the time

being at least, with England. Term was ended. Her parents were now in Rome, and perhaps sensing some unexplained *mal de vivre* in their daughter were anxious for her to join them. Who was it who'd written so persuasively about the homeland and the country of exile, about losing touch so decisively with either side (more precisely, with either side of the Atlantic) that one was a stranger finally to both? Well, she would re-solder the American connection, maybe travel back with them to the US and test the strength of it.

She spent her last night in London with Breeze, as ever impressed by her friend's swanky accommodation in an already swanky Hampstead. Breeze's father was a Hollywood lawyer, her mother a shrink to movie stars. Could Hadley really begrudge her friend such a luxurious inheritance? Hell no. Wouldn't she have jumped at the chance of a future without crippling student loans to pay off? Hell yes. A future, unlike her own, where she could always be bailed out financially and, meanwhile, live in the purple?

Hadley woke up next to Breeze, who was snoring lightly. If they occasionally shared the same bed – usually when one had stayed too late at the other's apartment and couldn't face the grim prospect of making the long trip home (in some cartographic paraphrase of their East Coast/West Coast polarity,

Hadley had always lived in South London, Breeze in the North) – they would sleep together in an entirely non-sexual camaraderie. How come, Hadley sometimes wondered, guys could never do this – or even understand it?

Hadley had packed the night before. When the taxi driver to the airport buzzed their apartment she was ready to go. Kissing the still-sleeping Breeze softly on the cheek, she let herself out. It was pretty cold down in the street, with a filigree of mist. The smiling Asian cabbie helped her put her bags in the trunk.

She got it just as she settled into the back seat. It was Nathaniel Hawthorne. And only a good time later, back in Pittsburgh, would she be able to locate the full quotation:

"...*The years, after all, have a kind of emptiness when we spend too many of them on a foreign shore. We defer the reality of life, in such cases, until a future moment, when we shall again breathe our natural air; but, by and by, there are no future moments; or, if we do return, we find that the native air has lost its invigorating quality, and that life has shifted its reality to the spot where we have deemed ourselves only temporary residents. Thus, between two continents, we have none at all, or only that little space of either in which we finally lay down our discontented bones. It is wise, therefore, to come back betimes, or never.*"

Hey, thought Hadley, even now speeding towards Heathrow, she should check it out, stick it on a postcard and send it as some sort of lame apology to Simon. Wasn't he, like her, a collector of such cute reflections? Wasn't that his 'sort of thing'? But where was Simon now?

Zac parked the Bentley fast and none too neatly on a sloping Hampstead back street.

It had not been difficult to get Breeze's address. He'd simply rung up the Theatre Department of her college, announced his name to the secretary and fed her some line about forwarding information pertaining to his next production. It was Breeze herself – in T-shirt and panties but already wearing mascara – who opened the front door to the maisonette.

"Where is she?" he asked without ceremony and before a startled Breeze could answer charged through, along the hallway and into her living room. "Well? Where is she?"

"Do you mean..."

"You know perfectly well who I mean. Where's Hadley?"

Without waiting for a reply, he strode through into the kitchen, the bathroom, the bedroom. Hadley was not there. Back in the living room, he turned to confront a still trembling Breeze.

"I asked you. Where is she?"

Breeze, regaining some sort of equilibrium, held out her hands, palms down, in a gesture of appeasement.

"Zac. I think you should sit down."

"Yeh? And then what?"

"Let me get you a drink."

"Okay. Double whiskey. No ice."

As Breeze moved to the kitchen, Zac threw himself in an armchair, one leg over its side, and stared hotly at the wall.

"Here." Breeze returned with the whiskey. "She's gone. She's gone to see her parents in Rome. They're over for a tour of Europe. They -"

"Yes. I know," he said curtly, shutting her off. He took a big gulp of his drink and refocused on the wall. A silence.

"You know? Listen..."

"You going to give me her address over there?"

"I'm not sure I should."

"Of course I already have her mobile number," he said defiantly.

"Then perhaps you should ask her yourself."

"Give me a break. She's on permanent voicemail." Again Zac gulped at his whiskey. Again a silence.

"Look," said Breeze. "Let's take this slowly. You want a refill?"

It was more than an hour later. Breeze felt exhausted. She had been fending off accusations, entreaties and threats all this time, most of them directed at the absent Hadley, occasionally at Breeze herself as the designated 'friend and protector'. Zac looked a wreck. He'd got through most of her Jack Daniels and now, exhausted himself, still slumped in the armchair, he seemed to her a figure more to be pitied than feared or despised. The corners of his eyes were wet and he seemed to Breeze all of a sudden terribly old and terribly fragile, the thumb of his left hand still manically stroking the ring on his little finger.

"Zac. What more can I say? What more can I do for you? I'm sorry."

Zac seemed slowly to gather himself. He sat forward, wiped his eyes and wearily attempted something like a smile. "I'm sorry too. It shouldn't be you dealing with all this. Thank you for the drink. Thank you for the" – he shrugged, finding the word – "consolation."

Suddenly Breeze felt nothing but compassion and sympathy.

"You can do one thing for me," said Zac, a shade ruefully.

"Which is?"

"Hold my hand?"

Breeze nodded. She moved over slowly, stood between his legs and took his hand, if only to stop his insistent stroking of the ring.

"Hey," he said softly, and reached up to kiss her.

Later that afternoon Tubs arrived in Hampstead by taxi. He was very excited. As if it might somehow disappear, he continued to fondle the little dark-blue velvet box in the right-hand pocket of his jacket. It contained a rather lovely ring. A big bouquet of flowers was on the seat next to him. If not now, then when, he asked himself?

He paid off the driver and stepped onto the road...

Naked and awake, Breeze lay across her bed. Pillows and duvet were strewn on the floor. She watched silently as Zac dressed himself and walked noiselessly out of the room. He was just releasing the inner lock on the front door, an old-fashioned design with the top half in bubbled glass enclosing a rose-design in dark blue and red, when a large, fuzzy shadow blocked out the light. Standing on the step, holding a bunch of flowers and looking up expectantly was a rather fat man, twenty years Zac's junior. Nodding curtly, Zac squeezed past, went down the steps and was gone.

Breeze heard her flat door click again. Irrationally perhaps, she had started to cry.

"Zac, listen. This has all been, like, a terrible mistake..." But looking up, she saw not Zac but Tubs who, normally pink-faced, was white with shock, his flowers now dangling absurdly from one hand.

"Breeze?"

Breeze sought to wipe away some mascara which had clotted her eyelashes. Now she started to weep again with a new and different shame and finally turned her smeared face to the pillow.

When, a good time later, her convulsive sobbing had eased she turned round, aware of how cold her still naked body was, splayed across the bed. The flat was empty. Tubs had gone.

Tubs spent the rest of the afternoon in what was, for him, a strange activity. He went to his tiny storeroom – the room at the back of his flat where he kept suitcases, long unused tennis racquets, an earlier generation of computer hardware – and pulled out the old battered trunk which had served him well through prep school, boarding school and university. In it were old school reports, mounted photographs of himself and his fellow sixth formers (was that really him in those days? So compact and with so much hair?), even some undergraduate essays. Dutifully, he put them in separate piles and in chronological order before tying each pile with string and then putting them back neatly in the trunk.

Moving to the bathroom, he took off all his clothes and contemplated himself with a certain distaste in the mirror. It seemed to him that he was already developing the breasts of elderly men who drink too much and take no exercise. As for the swollen stomach, he thought, as for the unprepossessing diminutive genitals beneath – well, let's not even contemplate those. Tubs began to reach for the medical cabinet where he kept his stash of anti-depressants... then paused.

Dammit. He'd give himself a proper bath and shave.

The water ran hot and copious into the tub, steaming up the mirror. He tested the temperature and turned off the taps. Contrary to his regular morning routine, he decided to shave first, but also decided that a double vodka – in the event a triple vodka – would be a comforting companion. He padded, naked, to the fridge, fixed himself the drink then padded back to the bathroom, glass in hand. Where was I? he asked himself.

Standing once more in front of the mirror, he massaged the shaving foam into his face and chins alike, then applied the razor. At the first stroke he slightly cut himself and contemplated the blood picked up on the end of his finger as one might some curious alien effluent. Again he looked at the full bath, himself in the clouded mirror, at the razor, at the blood.

Well well, he reflected, let the Antique Roman fall on his sword; let Modern Man fall on his Gillette.

"Nothing for me here," he declared out loud.

His house-cleaner found him in the bathtub the next morning. She said it was all a terrible mess.

Crossing the park for the last time that academic year, Simon was struck by how many people were smoking. Likewise, on the park's other side, in the streets of Kensington itself, he noted the increased number of shirt-sleeved individuals loitering in office doorways and lighting up. He was still getting over the small, intimate service of the week before that had marked the passing of Tubs. There had been no sign of Breeze, but there had been one or two colleagues there (including Nathalie) and the parents – the father in advanced stages of Parkinson's and shepherded by the mother who, bright-eyed, had told Simon he was her son's 'only true friend'. As perhaps he was, thought Simon. Poor fucker.

It was a routine of his to buy a take-away cappuccino at a local sandwich bar and carry it into class. It was only when he registered the absence of the bar's customary fug and dirty ashtrays that he understood. Of course! Today was the first day of Great Britain as an official 'smoke-free zone'. Those unrepentant nicotine addicts he'd seen all around had been flushed out of doors, and they could paradoxically now only feed their private craving in public non-enclosed spaces.

Simon shrugged. Well, he himself had quit just a couple of months before. In some ways it had been a symbolic letting-go of Hadley, love for whom had run co-extensive with his own resumed smoking. Now he was, so to speak, in a smoke-free zone all his own and wondering why he didn't feel better for it. Wasn't he now 'clean' where once he'd been 'down-and-dirty'? But then again, if love was a wound, wasn't it appropriate he should also have lesions on his lungs which bore it witness and which might, or might not, heal in due course? Only time would tell.

In a doorway opposite the entrance to his college, a couple of secretaries in thin blouses were smoking and gossiping. Simon marvelled at their resilience – clearly, they'd left their jackets inside despite the sharpness of this early-summer morning. Just looking at them, he felt a twinge of cold in his bones – and simultaneously remembered the refrain from an old Brecht play to which Hadley had once dragged him:

"See the smoke float free...
Into ever colder coldness."

Once inside, his lecture-notes spread before him, he allowed his students to settle. He was due to talk about the dark side of Modernism, about dissolution and despair, the breakdown of civilization and the self as experienced by a generation heading in its century's second decade for a conflict worse than any yet known to man. Why then did he suddenly feel so buoyant?

"Today we come to the last of my lectures." He looked up meaningfully. "And when I say 'the last' – I mean it!"

He did not know it, but later that afternoon Simon was aping the last hours of his good pal Tubs as he sat in the storeroom of his Bayswater flat, sorting out old papers, forgotten books, long-unused articles of clothing. Some of these latter he would take to the local charity shop where, in earlier days of *vache maigre*, he'd discovered them in the first place.

He showered and shaved. He had one last thing to do...

As, a little later, he eased past the skewed Japanese tree and up the forbidding steps with its guardian urns, he remembered the thrill of the very first time he'd done this. Sarah answered the door, looking, Simon thought, rather beautiful in her anticipation of sadness. They sat opposite each other on the angled sofas.

"So" she said finally, attempting a brave smile. "You've decided?"

"It was you always told me I never took decisions. That I was always deferring..." He reached across and took her hand. "Listen..."

"Don't say it, Simon."

"Say what?"

"That we'll always be friends?"

"But we will!"

"I've heard that rather often in my life. God forgive me," she added with a joyless little laugh, "I've even said it myself."

Simon, pre-empted in anything he might express, reached for the huge carrier-bag he'd brought with him. "I thought you might like these."

She spilled it out on the low glass coffee table. There were some fifty or so CDs. Ry Cooder, Van Morrison, Randy Newman. Portuguese *fado*. Argentine tangos. French chansons. It looked suddenly as if she might cry.

"You're not joining the Trappists, are you?" she asked gamely.

"No. Just going away for a while."

"How long's a while?"

He shrugged with an apologetic smile and sat beside her, hugging her tightly. Now she was crying a little, but embarrassed to show it. Seeking some momentary distraction, she wiped a cheek and picked up one of the CDs at random. On its case Simon had conscientiously listed in florid blue ink track titles, running lengths, date of recordings and names of supporting instrumentalists. *Ever the bloody professor*, she sighed privately.

"You know something? The first time I saw Zac's handwriting I thought I could never love a man with such a tight, mean way of writing. Yours, however... "And again she buried her face in his shoulder.

When Simon had eventually gone, she found under a pile of glossy magazines the copy of Colette she'd always meant to finish last time round. She flicked ruefully through it to where she'd left off reading: the ageing Léa with her self-awareness, her heroic renunciation of further fleshly pleasures... But almost immediately she cast the book aside. What a strange mixture of claptrap and truth it now seemed to her. Today's sixty was the new forty.

That evening she booked a flight to Dubai, two weeks in a five-star hotel and, for the next day, an appointment with her masseur.

Zac wanted to fly but could not. However hard he struggled upwards, pushing his palms out like everyone else, the ground seemed to suck him back down again. Others around him seemed to be having no such problems; already they were up there, smiling at him with a scarcely-concealed pity (wasn't that oily bugger Robert Donniger among them?), the men's coat tails flapping slightly, the ladies' ball gowns fluttering flirtatiously above their ankles and calves. Zac made one last, monumental effort, almost jumping into the air, but it was no good... and woke up bathed in sweat. Strangely, he had the feeling the dream had been in no way sexual.

Later that morning, pounding round the park, he felt the pull of a muscle in his left leg but tried to ignore it. Hey, why not look on the bright side? he asked himself. With just a sprinkle of good luck, everything might yet turn out okay. Once back home he would tell Iris he didn't want to live with her any more. He would bring Hadley back from wherever she was, kicking and screaming if need be. He would see Sarah and his daughter and, explaining that things hadn't worked out with Iris, would simultaneously offer money (the 'sixty-forty' previously withdrawn) and beg forgiveness, and – not, of course, mentioning Hadley – would ask if they could not start again, his maybe doing penance for a while by sleeping on the living-room couch. After all, he'd say a little plaintively, I need somewhere to sleep and I can scarcely throw Iris out just like that. For Heaven's sake, I'm not a monster, am I?

At about the same time that morning Mark, who had arrived early at his office, was coming to his own conclusions. Why not go round to Zac's and just thump the bastard? He'd been longing to do so for over twenty years now. He picked up his car keys, trying to remember the Worm's new address, that fuck-flat in Islington where he'd gone to live with his Irish bimbo. Yes. Why not? he asked himself again. One good pop on the nose and imagine the satisfaction he'd derive!

Also at this time Iris was clearing her desk, literally and metaphorically. Could Zac get her a new commission? she wondered. Without his support and a promise to produce any new play, she was probably scuppered. Her agent – as it happened a former literary manager to Zac's company before she turned gamekeeper – was notoriously ambitious, and fashion-conscious to boot. Would Iris be 'let go' if the association with Zac ever faltered? Perhaps she should diversify into TV or film? When he was back from his jogging she'd ask him.

Turning over some papers (Zac's rehearsal schedule, a bank statement, a credit-card bill) she saw he'd left his mobile behind and, like a child whose parents have gone out for the day leaving wardrobes and drawers to be delightfully explored, flicked it open. There were quite a few Outbox messages. Let's have a look at Zac's private life, she thought on a mischievous whim...

Her smile soon faded. "H. I love you with all my heart. Please contact me." "H. I can't live without you. Please please call." " H. Why are you doing this?" "H. Please call. We need to talk." "H. It's you and you only I have ever loved. Why won't you speak to me?"

Iris sat down heavily on the edge of the bed. Fuck. These messages were not for her. But then who were they for? Who in God's name was 'H.'? Had Iris all this time been living in a fool's paradise?

As Zac jogged towards the exit from the park he felt in pretty good shape. Yes, things would surely work out and, God knows, he'd weaselled his way out of tighter spots than these. Didn't he deserve – Guy's word – some 'gratification'? He worked like a Trojan. Why shouldn't he play like a Greek?

Slowing his pace to cross the road, he saw a silver car cruising by. Didn't he recognise it from somewhere?

But the car simply powered on, disappearing round a corner.

Zac stopped to catch his breath on the pavement outside his front door. The code! He'd forgotten the new code! In the same instant he also realised he'd forgotten his mobile too. Wearily he climbed the steps and tried punching in a number, but there was no answering click. He tried again, this time reversing the two last digits. Again no response. He'd just given up, resolving to buzz Iris, when again the car loomed into his peripheral vision, slowing as it passed.

Isn't that Mark's? he asked himself belatedly. But, if so, why on earth was the guy circling like this – some silver-charioted stalker, some hovering Nemesis?

Later, Zac would recall that in the first hot flush of an obscure panic he had felt something click inside him, though, turning, he would find it was no more than a downstairs neighbour – burly, amiable – releasing the lock from the door's other side before venturing out for his morning constitutional.

Zac glanced backward a last time – ah! the street was empty once more! – and, smiling as he let his neighbour pass, promptly fell over.

"You all right, old man?"

"Sure," grunted Zac, embarrassed. "Must have overdone it a bit."

Still smiling weakly, he eased past, walked up the

stairs to the first landing... and then fell over again. It was all most peculiar; he felt no pain, on the contrary a sense of peaceful detachment. Except now he could not get up. What was happening?

Zac groaned. "Fuck. Just when I was needing a pee..."

Five minutes later Iris found him, a circle of urine darkening his crotch, seated still on the first-floor landing, and looking, she thought, as helpless as a child. But a child who had aged ten years in as many minutes.

News of Zac's stroke travelled fast, reaching Hadley just as she was boarding a plane from Pittsburgh to New York, where she'd arranged to rent an apartment. A fellow student from her old class rang her with this and other 'gossip' from London. Hadley tried to contact Breeze but couldn't get a reply.

Fuck. A stroke. Hadley could not prevent herself from imagining just how this might have played out had she still been with him. What would she have done? What would have been the consequences between them? Would she have felt morally bound to stay by him, to hold his hand, to nurse him? And for how long?

Oddly, she thought of ringing Simon. But where was Simon now? And what could he do?

Fuck. Fuck. Fuck.

So Hadley mused throughout the short flight, unable to read or doze.

Simon stood on the deck of a steamer trailing up the Ionian Sea through morning mist as pale as winter breath on a plate of glass. He'd been travelling for some time now, principally by boat and train, and was beginning to lose track of where he'd been to and where he was going next, knowing only that here on the edge of Europe was some kind of limit, a place where myths and histories accumulated richly before toppling over into other continents, other cultures.

This particular island ahead, didn't it have something to do with Ulysses? (Then again, thought Simon with a sigh, didn't they all have something to do with Ulysses?) 'Kerkira' they called it and now, bunched between two shapeless mounds revealing themselves as hilltop forts, the silhouettes of lemon trees and orange trees were stepping out to greet him. The clouds shifted and the water turned from a uniform opal to polished dark facets of green and blue, while the black windsock of shoreline houses changed to one winking, smiling swathe of stucco.

Simon, now practically alone on deck, reckoned

he liked what he saw. "Yes," he told himself, already reaching for his Ray-Bans. "This place I could get to know. This place will do. For a while."

Epilogue

A little over two years later Hadley walked down London's Southampton Row feeling like an alien from another planet or, more precisely, a *revenante* who, returning to her old haunts, finds nothing has changed – except she is now invisible and the world has forgotten her.

It was a beautiful Spring morning. Hadley paused at the odd window display, but every store here seemed to be selling computers, cameras or sound systems, stuff she could get back home in abundance, and she turned left down a side street. What did they call this area? Surely Bloomsbury was further east. Fitzrovia perhaps? She walked on.

Hadley was three months pregnant. Back in New York, Richard had urged her to indulge her whim and visit London again. Who could say, with the child once born, when she'd have another such opportunity?

She had married Richard a year or so before. He was very tall, rather handsome (so at least Hadley thought) and a company lawyer. When she had first entered his pleasant apartment on the Upper East Side she had spontaneously laughed out loud and felt obliged to explain to him that there was nothing especially comic about it, simply that it had "felt so right". What could she have meant? She had no idea – except he also was 'so right' and made her happy. They had met when Hadley, having finally renounced all further academic pursuits, was just finishing the run of an old Neil LaBute play off-Broadway. She had been introduced to him by a fellow actress who'd announced *sotto voce* that he was "possibly the last honest attorney in New York" and "probably a marvellous fuck too". Well, in due course Hadley would come to find that Richard lived up to that estimate on both counts and was great fun into the bargain. (Almost immediately after her pronouncement the actress-friend had moved out West; Hadley had never had the chance to congratulate her on her acuity.)

Hadley came out of a dank passageway and into the sunlight of Queen's Square, which she remembered as always liking for its Italian hospital and that strange little school, its entrance perched on high, where they ran classes for adults in Creative Writing, Painting and much else. She sat down. Here in the more floral part of the square she was alone except for a pair of tanned and grizzled winos on the next bench along, who were opening with relish what appeared to be their first extra-strength lagers of the day.

Where was Simon now? she wondered. A postcard received some months earlier suggested he was on a Greek island, but had that been a holiday or something more permanent? She smiled as she remembered his Theory of the Sabbatical —'once surrendered, never recovered'. Well, had he 'surrendered' too, quit academia for a life of lotus-eating? If so, how did he live? By teaching English Literature to Greek shepherds and goat-boys? It remained a mystery.

Breeze was back on the West Coast and had visited them in New York in the last days of winter. A familiar story. On arrival she had entertained Hadley and Richard enormously with a list of the outrageous downtown clubs she was going to hit – "hetero, homo, and anything in between" – only to back out when neither of her hosts seemed impatient to accompany her. "Hey, I'm a married woman now," Hadley had protested with a laugh, "and banged up too! For me it's like smoking – a thing of the past. But why not go solo?" Breeze had shaken her head and changed the subject. There was only the briefest – and saddest – of pauses in remembrance of Tubs.

And then, finally, there was Zac...

Hadley got word of him from time to time. Because of the stroke – he remained wheelchair-bound – his career was severely curtailed, but he still had some kind of continuance. Once, the same fellow student who'd telephoned her with news of Zac's stroke had emailed a newspaper profile of him and Iris, a profile celebrating how his illness and her caring for him had 'only deepened that exclusive and all-defining love they'd known for each other from the start'. Was it a buried memory of that article (Hadley hadn't wished to be reminded of Zac and had deleted it straight away) which had nevertheless led her footsteps in this direction? Nearby, as she recalled, was the hospital for neurological disorders where he had been in rehab, returning there off and on ever since, according to the newspaper. Hell, she thought, may they glean such happiness as they can, and rose from her bench...

Only to sit right down again, cursing her foolishness. Negotiating the ramp up to the hospital entrance were a youngish, dark-haired woman and a man in a wheelchair. The man seemed flustered or irritated or both, brushing away the woman's protective hand as if to say he could manage on his own. But Hadley was seeing all this from some forty yards off, their backs were towards her and she couldn't swear to their identities. Surely, she thought, Fate wouldn't play so gross a hand on this her rare visit back to London?

She decided to take no chances. Leaving the square from another angle, she followed a cobbled little side-street which wound past a shop selling Rare Books in French and German, a traditional English pub with coach lamps outside, and a trattoria called Bella Italia which was just opening for lunch.

Ah, Europe! thought Hadley with a private smile. How sweet! How innocent! And she continued on her way.

BV - #0175 - 220426 - C0 - 203/127/17 - PB - 9781861519184 - Matt Lamination